"*Lost Girl* is a compulsive thrill-ride that reads as if it's been pulled straight from the headlines. Kammier's journalism background brings undeniable authenticity to a novel that has it all—a love story, a murder mystery, and a real-life introduction into the distinctive world of television news."

—CAROLINE MITCHELL,
New York Times Best-Selling Author

"An unstoppable, YA Romantic Suspense, full of secrets and lies. *Lost Girl* is a whodunnit that will keep you riveting until the very last page."

—ROBERT KOVACIK,
Anchor/Reporter at NBC Los Angeles

"Great storytelling in a beautiful and off-the-beaten-path part of America. I read it cover-to-cover in one sitting and loved every minute of it. *Lost Girl* made me recall my earliest days as a reporter chasing a serial killer!"

—SHANE BISHOP,
National Producer for a Primetime Crime Show

MORE PRAISE FOR
Lost Girl, A Shelby Day Novel

"Holly Kammier has crafted a first-rate romantic suspense story, with wonderfully realized characters who will grip your interest until the very end. In fierce, young Shelby Day, Kammier has created a heroine both utterly familiar and entirely modern, a figure to root for (and hold your breath for) page after page."

—HUGO SHWYZER,
Contributor to *Jezebel*, *The Atlantic*, *Salon*,
and Co-Author of *Beauty, Disrupted: A Memoir*,
A Biography of Supermodel Carré Ottis

"Ambition. Betrayal. Envy. Romance. And a fledgling TV news reporter hell-bent on tracking down a killer in a double homicide even as she struggles to resist the added complication of falling for the one person who sees beyond her bravado. *Lost Girl, A Shelby Day Novel* from Holly Kammier, will lure you into this fast-paced, edge-of-your-seat tale from the get-go, leaving you craving more from this talented writer. In a nutshell, 5-stars!"

—LAURA TAYLOR,
6-Time Romantic Times Award Winning Author

LOST GIRL

Debbie
Happy Reading! ♡
may you be up and
walking soon ;)

LOST GIRL

A SHELBY DAY NOVEL

by

HOLLY KAMMIER

ACORN
PUBLISHING

FROM THE TINY ACORN...
GROWS THE MIGHTY OAK

This is a work of fiction. References to real people, events, establishments, organizations, or locales are intended only to provide a sense of authenticity and are used fictitiously. All other characters, and all incidents and dialogue are drawn from the author's imagination and are not to be construed as real.

Cover design by Damonza
Author photo by Julia Badei of Studio Bijou
Interior design by Debra Cranfield Kennedy

ISBN-13: 978-1-947392-61-8 (hardcover)

ISBN-13: 978-1-947392-57-1 (paperback)

This book is for Josh, Aiden, and Alex.

And my fearless goddaughter,
who asked me to write a story about a girl named Shelby.

PROLOGUE

This was the story that was going to change my life. A breaking news report so shocking, it sounded more like a horror movie than reality. The kind of tale I'd made up various versions of and played out in my head enough times, I was certain it could never possibly happen.

Now it was real. I was in the middle of it—tied to a chair with blood dripping down my temple—and I doubted I'd be alive long enough to tell anyone . . .

CHAPTER ONE

"Shelby, take two steps to your left. I want to get the mountains in the background behind the crime scene." Jack pushed his long, dark hair from his face and adjusted the angle on the news camera.

I shuffled my feet a few inches to give him a better view of the jagged Siskiyou range flanking our small Oregon town. "Better?"

"A little farther."

Taking another side-step, my warm breath clouded in the early-morning chill. "How do I look?" I asked.

This was the kind of breaking news story that would get me noticed as a real investigative reporter, and Jack was the type of friend who would tell me if I appeared as panicked as I felt.

He tilted his head in thought before he nodded. "You look perfect."

"Thanks," I said, grateful to have him on my side. Reminding myself to enunciate each word, I swept aside my bangs, damp with nervous perspiration, and stared into the television camera's dark lens.

"And you're live in three, two . . ." Our director counted down in my earpiece while the news anchor in studio finished introducing my story. Jack pointed his index finger at me to indicate we were on air.

I swallowed hard, the familiar shake of anxiety slicing through my bones. "Lacey, it's a crime so devastating it could've been ripped straight from a Shakespearean tragedy. Two young women are dead. The victims were stabbed repeatedly by an intruder who crept inside their Ashland home while they slept. And it all happened right here on Halloween night."

Pivoting toward the brick two-story Craftsman behind me, I gripped my microphone tighter. The pressure helped steady me. "One of the women in this double homicide is rumored to be a crowned beauty queen. She and her room-mate were murdered inside their seemingly safe Belle Street address, only a couple blocks south of Briscoe Elementary School. The biggest questions this morning are, who broke into this quiet suburban home in the middle of the night . . . and why would someone want to kill these two women?"

Shivering at the horror of it all, I turned back to the camera. "Lacey, we'll be updating viewers on this developing story as details emerge. Live in Ashland, I'm Shelby Day, *NBC 4 News.*"

As the magnitude of the crime settled into my already tense shoulders, I waited for Jack to point his index finger again, this time giving me the "clear sign" that we were off air. Police had arrived on the scene only a few hours ago, and none of the other news outlets in town were here yet. This was my chance to get a jump on interviews.

"Hey, Jack." I tugged out my earpiece and dug in my

handbag for my cellphone with shaking hands. "Can you get some exterior shots of the scene while I ask the cops some questions? I can't believe we're the only ones covering this. Don't they listen to the police scanners? What's the holdup?"

"Waiting for the bodies to cool?" Jack, a Southern California surfer-boy transplant, raised his eyebrows at me.

"Come on. It's okay for us to be here." My insides shook as I spoke. "This is our job. Hurry and get as many shots as you can." It was important to act as if I had it all together—even if I didn't.

"You got it." He swiveled the camera on the tripod and zoomed in on a man in white coveralls and purple gloves leaving the house.

"Shoot, there's Becca Barnes," I whispered under my breath, eyeing up the gangly brunette heading our way. She carried her news camera in one hand while a fake Louis Vuitton dangled from her free shoulder. Becca looked from the scene to Jack and back again, as if she couldn't decide which was her priority. Serving as a watchdog for society was clearly not her only passion.

I held my ground. If she stopped to say "hello" to Jack, I could approach the cops without her sniffing over my shoulder and stealing my info. Sure enough, she waved at Jack. He paused from shooting to say "hi."

Jack was too polite for journalism.

I headed to the other edge of the frost-bitten lawn, creeping as close to the front door as the crime scene tape allowed. A tall bald man dressed in jeans and a navy-blue police jacket stepped outside the home and onto the wrap-around porch. This was my chance.

The man stood a good half-foot taller than most of his colleagues and held himself with the confidence of a man in charge.

"Excuse me, sir." I straightened my knee-length red cardigan as I leaned over the yellow tape. "Officer?"

"Sergeant Dunbar. What can I do for you?" He strode down the tidy wooden porch steps and walked toward me.

"I have a few quick questions."

"Off camera?" His eyes scanned the sidewalk, his gaze landing on Becca and Jack.

"Sure, if that's what you'd like." I bit the inside of my cheek, intent on convincing him to give me an on-camera interview. First, I'd warm him up with some questions. "Can you briefly tell me what you know so far?"

"What's your name? You look familiar."

"Shelby Day, I'm with *NBC 4 News.*"

"That's right." He tapped his thumb over his trimmed mustache. "I've seen you around."

"I've been here about ten months. I report the crime stories." I doubted he really remembered any of my news coverage.

Ashland was a thriving community, known mostly for its renowned Shakespeare Festival and quaint liberal arts college. While a good majority of people filling the streets were either tourists or Southern Oregon University students, working as a television reporter did make it difficult to go unrecognized among the locals. Still, with my brown hair, brown eyes, and average looks, I didn't exactly stand out from the other Ashland journalists.

"You covered the child prostitution court case," Sergeant Dunbar interrupted my thoughts.

I winced at the memory of such a painful story. "That was me."

He stared right into my eyes. "You also covered the funeral for one of our young officers killed in the line of duty." He took another look over at Becca and Jack before returning his gaze back to me. "You get the facts straight. Most of these newbie reporters boggle it up. What can I help you with?"

"Can you tell me what you know so far?" My thumb hovered over my phone, ready to type in all the details.

Sergeant Dunbar lifted his head. "The first victim was a twenty-two-year-old Caucasian female. We're not releasing details on the second victim until the family's been notified."

My eyes followed Sergeant Dunbar's, catching sight of two men donning black coroner's office jackets. They carried a gurney, removing one of the dead girls. A blue sheet covered her body, but sticking out, I saw a single big toe, her nail-polish a blushing shade of pink.

Feeling vulnerable, I stood up straighter, trying to stretch my five-foot-two body as tall as I could make it. Those dead girls were near my age, and just like me, living on their own far from home. This could have been me or any of my friends. It was hard not to feel a connection, and it made me want to work even harder to gather as much information as possible.

After making sure Jack was pointing the news camera in the coroners' direction, I rounded back my shoulders and inhaled deep, turning back to Sergeant Dunbar. "We heard over the scanner that one of the two victims was Melissa Rossi. Our assignment editor is friends with her aunt. I understand Melissa was originally from the Crater Lake area and she lived here with two other girls. One of the roommates was a former beauty queen from the East Coast."

"I can't comment on that at this time."

"What is the name of the third roommate, the one who survived?"

"We're not going to release the names of any of the victims at this time."

"Who's the primary suspect?" I asked.

"We don't have one yet."

"Could it be the third roommate?"

"I can't comment on that either. We need to gather more evidence before we can speculate or make any assumptions."

I scanned the scene for any clues as to what I should ask the detective next. The picturesque Craftsman tucked against the mountains betrayed none of the dark secrets held inside. Men and women, some in the Ashland PD uniform, some not, moved in and out of the front door. A law enforcement officer carrying a camera walked across the wet lawn toward the sidewalk and ducked under the crime tape.

"What happened in there?" I asked.

Sergeant Dunbar's brows lowered along with his voice. "Last night, the victims were handing out Halloween candy to trick-or-treaters. They went to bed in their individual rooms around 10:30 p.m. The two victims slept in adjacent bedrooms.

"At approximately 2 a.m., an unidentified man entered the house and went upstairs. Witnesses said they woke up to the sound of screaming in the house. When they went to see what was going on, they saw the silhouette of a man bolting out of the house.

"There's evidence that suggests the assailant fled through a back window. After several minutes, the witness found the two victims lying on the floor unresponsive. They were both covered in blood with multiple stab wounds. By the time police and paramedics arrived, both women were dead."

"How do you know the attacker was a man?" I asked.

"They saw his silhouette."

I figured the "witnesses" he was referring to must be the third roommate. Sergeant Dunbar was probably hiding her identity for her protection. But how could we know she was telling the truth about what she saw? I made a note for myself to dig deeper.

Then I thought of another angle, the dozens of unbathed men and women dressed as hippies who hung out in small groups on the sidewalks all over downtown smoking weed and playing banjos and flutes for donations. "Do you think this murder has anything to do with the expanding transient population along Main Street? A lot of people think they're dangerous."

Sergeant Dunbar looked around before responding just above a whisper. "Off the record, it doesn't appear to be a burglary. As far as we know, nothing was stolen. This looks personal. We're still gathering evidence."

"Thank you so much, Sergeant. Are you sure I couldn't ask you a few basic questions on camera, so we can let the public know what to do? This is a small town. People are going to be terrified that a serial killer may be on the loose." I held my breath as I waited for his response. An interview with the lead detective would give this story the weight it deserved. I silently prayed for a "yes".

Sergeant Dunbar ran his finger over his mustache once again and a took in a deep breath. Another cop called out to him with questions before he turned back to me and nodded his approval.

"Jack," I called, waving him over before the sergeant changed his mind.

After the interview, as we packed our gear and headed to the news van, Jack looked over at me with a glimmer of pride. "You really did a great job, Shelby."

"Thanks." I fiddled with my phone as Jack placed his camera in the trunk.

"I'm serious. I know I give you a hard time for being so determined, but you showed your force as a journalist and you earned the right to carry this story."

My eyes met his. I mouthed a thank-you.

Jack took the tripod from my hand and placed it next to the camera. "Not bad for the little rich girl from LA who nobody expected to stand on her own or make a difference."

His words made me swell with pride. It was everything I wanted to believe. But what I didn't know then, what I couldn't have known, was that my blind pursuit to become a better person would threaten to strip away all the things that mattered most to me.

I had already set in motion my path to destruction.

CHAPTER TWO

Back at the news station, I sat in front of a pair of side-by-side computer screens in a dimly lit, long, narrow editing bay reviewing Jack's footage. He stepped behind me, looking over my shoulder.

"Hey, Shelby, what do you think?" he asked.

I tugged on my earlobe as I scrolled through the video. "Great shots. But there're so many unanswered questions. I have already pounced on Carolyn at the assignment desk and grilled her about everything she knows."

"Way to make friends," he said with a smile, but I knew he meant to poke at me.

I bit my lip, intent on appearing tough. "A good reporter asks questions." There was no reason to feel ashamed. Carolyn, with her sweet smile and humble gray-haired bob, had grown up in Ashland. She knew everybody in town. And she was our assignment editor. It was her job to fill us in on everything she knew.

"Anyway," I continued, "I guess the girls who lived there were friendly with each other, but Melissa had beef with the beauty queen. Apparently, Ms. Alabama, or whatever title she held, hooked up with every guy in town. It got so bad that Melissa and the other roommate had been talking about kicking out 'Miss Congeniality'."

Jack's fingers brushed against my left shoulder as he rested his hands on the back of my chair. Warmth radiated throughout my body like an involuntary spark of electricity.

"Do you think the roommates went after the beauty queen and something went wrong and Melissa Rossi also got killed?" Jack asked, stepping away from me as I swiveled my chair around.

I rubbed the back of my neck. "If the murderer wasn't some random rapist who got caught in the act, I guess it's possible. Seems kind of wild, but people are crazy. I wish we knew for sure who the second victim was, it would help us form a clearer theory. I went deep in Melissa Rossi's Instagram trying to find pictures of her roommates and screenshotted a bunch of her photos, but she never tagged anybody, so I can't be sure who is who."

"Yeah?"

"It kind of made my stomach hurt looking at her smiling at the camera, knowing she's dead."

Jack leaned the length of his solid six-foot frame against the wall of the editing bay. "Admit it, you're as soft as me."

Unlike so many of our colleagues, Jack knew I had to fight to maintain a detached professional indifference to the stories I covered. His unabashed compassion for others seeped into me, making it even harder. And that was dangerous in this line of work.

Just like a good cop, firefighter, or emergency room doctor, if a journalist opened up their heart while covering hard news, it made room for other feelings to creep inside.

Sorrow, fear, outrage. Any one of those emotions challenged a reporter's ability to present an unbiased story. Not to mention emotional burnout.

Story after story, crime after crime, accident after accident, we were some of the first people on the scene. It was imperative to remain neutral. Follow protocol. Numb our emotions in order to get the job done properly.

"What'd she look like?" Jack asked.

I blinked my eyes, thinking. "Melissa Rossi?" I picked up my phone to show him. "She was cute. Not pretty, but sweet-looking. Real petite, curly orangey-red hair, pale, lots of freckles. But mostly, she looked so . . . alive."

Jack's broad shoulders slumped as he scrolled through her photos. His blue eyes wandered to someplace far away. "I feel so bad for her family."

I turned back toward the computer screens to keep him from seeing the sadness I felt hearing his words. "She was the same age as you, twenty-two. A year older than me. Can you imagine only having one more year to live?"

When Jack didn't say anything back, I scrolled forward on the video. He'd taken some heartbreaking shots, an up-close picture of a deflated smiling canvas pumpkin no longer welcoming enthusiastic trick-or-treaters on the hunt for candy. A blue coroner's logo marked the back of a white transportation van, parked and ready to haul away dead bodies on this gloomy gray morning. I stared at the deep footprints left by investigators across the front lawn's thick layer of wet autumn leaves. Next came a wide shot. Two men rolled out the metal gurney carrying a victim, the one with the pink toenail polish.

The newsroom's air-conditioning kicked on, cooling

the overheated equipment in the editing bay, and blasting a musty frigid breeze down my shoulders. I reminded myself to stay focused on the facts.

Carolyn had told me Melissa had graduated from OSU and immediately landed a job with the Jackson County Health Department as a health inspector. Maybe one of the restaurant owners was seeking revenge. A bad rating could destroy someone's business.

Or, the murders could have had nothing to do with Melissa at all. Maybe she was just a girl living in the wrong house at the wrong time. Rubbing the middle of my forehead, I said to Jack, "What if one of the beauty queen's ex-friends-with-benefits went over to kill her, and Melissa Rossi got in his way? Or maybe they were part of some twisted satanic cult killing? This did happen on Halloween."

Jack looked at the ground beneath his feet. "Whatever happened, no one deserves to die like that."

I shook my head trying to erase my grief for the two young victims. "We need to know more."

"Well, it's gonna have to wait. The cops probably aren't going to release anything else today and Carolyn asked me to tell you she has another assignment for you. She wants you to edit what you've got for tonight's show and move on to another story."

"What? Can't she assign that stuff to another reporter? This is the biggest news we'll probably get all year. This is *Dateline* shit, Jack. Everyone in town is going to be terrified and want to know more. I'll go talk to her." I paused the video and stood up.

He frowned. "Why can't you let it go for a few hours?"

"A killer is free, someone might know something that

could help catch him . . . or her. You don't let that go for a few hours. Besides, let's be smart, this is the kind of story that could bounce a girl back home to Los Angeles a whole lot faster."

Covering an on-going story with the potential for national exposure was résumé-building material that opened doors in top-paying, highly respected, big city newsrooms. No more carrying around heavy camera equipment on any story that wasn't live. No more spending my days working a new angle on the annual Pear Blossom Parade or fun ways to repurpose your Halloween pumpkins.

I could nab a job closer to my family and make my dad proud. Becoming a successful journalist was as much his dream for me as it was my own. I was doing this for both of us.

"So, it's all about you." Jack crossed his arms.

"No." I could feel the heat rising in my face. "Why are you so noble? You're a photojournalist. I'm a television reporter. This is our chance to cover something real. Aren't you tired of shooting video on craft festivals and the latest skate park? Don't you want more?"

"What if those are the things that really matter? Why can't the little things in life be important to you, too?"

Jack's mellow vibe was the reason I pushed away my attraction for him. He could derail my career if I let him and, considering all the flawed choices I'd made in my teen years, I refused to allow anything to derail my goals. Standing on my own and helping others meant the world to me.

"Jack, no one gets into this business to cover the soft stories." I squeezed past him in the tight pathway of the darkened editing bays and headed toward the assignment desk's bright lights and bleeping scanners.

A sense of urgency locked me in its grip. I was going to cover this story wherever it led, until the very end.

CHAPTER THREE

Saturday morning, I sat in the nearly empty newsroom bouncing my leg in anxiety and stalking a profile on Instagram for the hundredth time. Anything to distract myself from the terrifying note I'd found on my front door this morning.

Trying to calm my nerves, I told myself it was nothing I couldn't handle and took a sip of chamomile tea. The steam curled in white vapor ribbons from the rim of my NBC peacock mug. As good as it felt to hold a warm cup, the chamomile's apple flower scent and earthy sweet taste weren't helping fast enough.

Again, I checked the clock, antsy for Jack to show up. He was five minutes late and he'd insisted I wait for him. I decided to give him ten more minutes before I packed up the camera bag and took off on my own.

Yesterday, less than twenty-four hours after the murders, police had knocked on a front door one block away from the victim's house. Melissa Rossi's on-again, off-again boyfriend, Alex Haskell answered the door. My assignment editor held me back from jumping on the story, but our news director gave me permission to spend my two off days over the weekend working on it. I'd already made contact with the now off-again boyfriend through Instagram and set up an interview with him.

"Shelby," Jack's deep voice reverberated against the entrance of the newsroom's long empty hallway. "This place is dead. You ready to roll?"

I peeked over my computer monitor with a nervous laugh. "Welcome to the weekend at *NBC 4 News*, where the staff is low and morale is lower." The weekend crew in a small-town newsroom was on the lowest rungs of the ladder from the big leagues.

When Jack smiled at me, the sexy scar that traced from the seam of his lip to the curve of his chin, tilted ever so slightly. He could pass for one of the movie stars cruising the LA streets where I grew up.

Warm brown skin the color of desert sand. Velvet blue eyes and high cheek bones that reflected his not-so-distant Native American blood. It was easy to get distracted, even as freaked out as I was. I reminded myself to stay focused on work and not crush on my best friend.

"Travis and Lily already took off?" he asked.

Looking around the newsroom, I remembered our weekend anchor and sports anchor were out working stories. "They left about an hour ago. You sure you want to do this on your day off? I'm fine going on my own."

"I'm not letting you interview a potential murderer without protection."

Protection. I bit at my thumb nail feeling my heartbeat thump faster. This morning, as I was heading out to check the mailbox before I left for work, I found a typed note taped to my front door.

> Congratulations Ms. Day.
> Your lead story was quite the coup.
> I'd advise quitting now while you're ahead . . .
> if I were you.

I'd nearly lost my breakfast when I read it.

"My knight in shining armor," I said sarcastically, crossing my arms and showing Jack my best game face.

Jack lowered his head and studied me, searching for the truth. "Something's on your mind."

"This interview," I said, gathering up my things. Jack didn't need to know about the note. I wasn't going to be scared into losing my lead story because of some creep, and I definitely didn't need anyone's protection. I could take care of myself just fine. "I'm actually glad you're coming along because you'll be able to get a good two-shot of me on camera interviewing Melissa's boyfriend. The bigger networks might pick it up."

"Bigger networks are more your speed, huh?" Jack looked over my shoulder. "Hey, Kaya." He nodded to our weekend assignment editor. "How's it going?"

Kaya, a bobbed blonde Southern Oregon University student beamed at Jack. "Good," she said to him. "Slow news day so I'm listening to the scanners and digging through social media posts to see what's going on around town."

"That's cool." Jack looked back at me. "I'll grab the keys to the news car and start loading. Wait for you out back?"

"Let me help." I stood up and shook off my nerves about

the note. This was an important interview and we had work to do. Fear was a waste of time.

———

Jack parked the news station's white Ford Fusion in front of Alex Haskell's cute single-story house, its small front yard bordered with well-tended, creamy white roses. A skinny hipster sporting thick black-rimmed glasses and a red and black flannel shirt sat on the front steps of the porch, eyes on his phone. This didn't seem like the kind of place a guy like him would live in—too nice. As we approached the front porch he folded and unfolded his arms across his chest. "Hey," he said. Morning sunshine reflected the light sheen of oil on his face.

Alex Haskell didn't look like a knife-wielding killer.

I smoothed out my knee-length gray dress and walked up to him with an extended hand. "Thanks for letting us come over."

"No problem." He squeezed his fingers into the flesh of his forearm before he reached out to shake my hand. "You actually gave me a second to breathe and process this before you asked me to talk. ABC had a reporter standing outside the police station yesterday waiting for me so she could come at me with questions. Another reporter came out of nowhere this morning and knocked on my front door. I appreciate you being so cool about this."

I thought of my disappointment when Carolyn had insisted I wait to track down Alex. Following orders had paid off.

"Anyway," he continued, "my parents are driving up

tonight, so you're the only reporter I'm talking to. My mom prefers I keep quiet until they get here. She'll probably hire a lawyer, which is pointless. As soon as my blood test results come back, everyone'll know it wasn't me."

I motioned to my partner. "This is Jack, he's going to shoot our interview. How long do you have to wait for the test results?"

"Probably about a month."

"That's a long time to live under a shadow," I said, trying to imagine how that would feel.

"I have nothing to hide. I just hope the police find the real killer. He needs to be locked up before he hurts anybody else." Alex turned his face away from me, as if he was trying to stop himself from crying.

I fought the reflex to reach out and comfort him. "I'm so sorry for your loss."

"Thanks." He rubbed at his eyes.

"Hey, man," Jack spoke up, no doubt trying to relieve some of the tension. "You mind if I grab some video of the outside of your home before we get started?"

"Won't that lead people to my house if they know what it looks like?"

"If news outlets are sending reporters here, I'm sure they already took footage," I said. "Besides, in a town this size, everyone's going to know where you live."

"All right. Be my guest." Alex stood up and shoved his free hand into his pants pocket, the other hand squeezing tight to his cell phone.

I pulled my thick black cardigan tighter in the morning chill. "Thanks. It helps when I'm editing your story to have video, that way the camera's not directly focused on us the whole time. Where do you want to do the interview?"

"Inside is good, next to the fireplace maybe." He pushed open the blue front door, the same door police had knocked on only yesterday to blast Alex with questions and notify him that his ex-girlfriend was dead.

I looked at Jack. "You can come in whenever you're ready."

Jack stepped to my side. "I'll get the exterior shots on our way out." My knight in shining armor wasn't going to let me go in alone. I had to admit, even if I could handle this, it was pretty sweet of him.

We slipped off our shoes, per Alex's request, and followed him into the house. The sunlit hallway led to a surprisingly spacious living room decked out with cherry hardwood floors, elaborate crown molding, and decorated in Tommy Bahama-style furniture. "Nice place." I set my bag on the floor next to a dark wood coffee table.

"Thanks. My parents live down in San Francisco and are hardly ever up here, so they let my brother and me room together. He just took off on a run to give us some space."

"How long have you lived in Ashland?"

"Almost two years now. My brother and I moved up after college for work. I met Melissa at *The Bar Fly* on First Street a few months ago. We were both hanging with friends and we just clicked."

I knew from Carolyn, Melissa Rossi had survived a life-threatening car crash when she was in high-school. Paramedics revived her on the scene after she was declared dead, but even then, with all her injuries, doctors thought she'd end up a vegetable, or at best, a paraplegic. Melissa battled like a warrior-woman, pushing herself through brutal physical therapy to take back her life. It was impossible not to admire her strength and courage. I felt a kinship with Melissa, we were both fighters, and I was eager to hear what Alex had to say about her.

While I discussed logistics with Alex, Jack carried two dining room chairs into the living room and set them in front of the electric fireplace. He went about getting his camera ready and gave me a hand signal when he was ready to go.

"Great." I took a seat in one of the chairs, still trying to shake off my nerves. This was an exclusive interview and I didn't want to waste the opportunity by overlooking any important questions. "Sit here."

Alex adjusted his jeans and sat down. Jack asked for his permission to turn on the fire to make everything look cozy. I handed Alex a lavalier mic and instructed him on how to string the thimble-sized microphone up his green sweater and attach it to the collar.

"We're recording," Jack said.

"Alex," I asked, sitting up straighter and tucking a strand of hair behind my ear. "Can we start with you saying and spelling your first and last name for us on camera? It helps identify you if anyone else needs to use our footage."

He pushed at the cuticle on his thumb and stared into the camera. "Sure, it's Alex Haskell. A–L–E–X H–A–S–K–E–L–L."

"Perfect. We're here with Melissa Rossi's ex-boyfriend," I said to the camera to clarify who Alex was in relation to the story. "Alex, look at me like we're having a real conversation, not at Jack or the camera."

"Okay." His eyes went wide and panicky.

"Don't worry, we're not live. If you stumble on your words, we can start over at any time. I'll edit this back at the station. Alex, can you tell me, do you know which other girl in the house was killed?"

"There's a lot of rumors, most people think it was Daphne, but no one knows for sure because the police aren't saying anything."

"Which one was Daphne?" I asked.

"She did pageants and worked for the Shakespeare Festival." He shrugged. "But some are positive it was Kathy. She's tough though, Kathy owned part of the *Four Maidens Bar and Grill* in Medford. She kicked out the drunks and attended all the community meetings and stuff where people would complain about having to deal with a bar in their neighborhood. Kathy likes to piss people off." Alex pursed his lips as his nose turned red.

"No one's heard from either one of them since Thursday?" I asked.

He shook his head.

"Alex, I know this is all very fresh for you, but could you tell me what happened to you on the morning of the murders?"

He rubbed his palms on his jeans. "I woke up yesterday to knocking on the front door. I looked out the peephole and nearly jumped backwards. There were at least five cops standing there. As soon as I opened the door, they asked if I had any weapons. It was really scary. I had no idea what was going on. I thought maybe someone had called them as a prank or something. Anyway, I told them I didn't have any weapons on me, the only thing I had was something I hid under my mattress for protection. One of the cops asked if they could come in. I wanted to keep things mellow, so I invited them inside."

"What kind of weapon did you have?"

His face flushed. "A knife. I always keep it where I sleep, just in case. One of the officers told me what happened to Melissa and asked me if I could come into the station for questioning. He also asked if they could take my knife in."

The flames in the electric fireplace flickered and swayed, its heat licking the glass enclosure. "You must have been completely shocked and destroyed by the news."

"I couldn't believe any of it was real."

I shifted my weight, preparing to dig deeper. "Was your brother home at the time?"

"No, he'd spent the night at a friend's. It was just me and the cops."

"I understand you and the victim, Melissa Rossi, saw each other on and off. Was it kind of a rocky relationship?"

"I guess." He cracked his knuckles. "We'd fight, break up, get back together. She'd say something to make me mad. I'd say something to hurt her. She wanted to get engaged. I wasn't ready for that, not marriage. I didn't even know if I loved her yet. I'm only twenty-three," he said, digging at nonexistent dirt under his fingernails.

I tilted my head to get back his attention. "I heard you'd been arguing for weeks."

"Yeah."

"What happened?" I asked.

"Melissa started seeing someone else. She said she needed to move on if I wasn't going to settle down. I think she was trying to make me jealous so I would take her back, but she started hooking up with the other guy so fast, it felt like she'd already been seeing him for a while. What was I supposed to think? Honestly, I feel bad about it now, but at the time, I was more pissed off than jealous."

I commanded myself to ask the next question, no matter how hard it was to sit face-to-face and make accusations. "Pissed off enough to hurt her?"

His eyes opened wide before narrowing with either pain or rage, I couldn't tell which. "I would never hurt a woman. Especially not Melissa. I'm not that kind of guy."

I looked back at him without speaking, holding my silence to make him uncomfortable, nudging him to fill the empty space with words he hadn't planned to speak.

Tears filled his eyes. "Melissa was a nice girl, I cared a lot about her. If we hadn't broken up, she probably would've been here with me."

"I have to ask, to clear the air. Where were you late Thursday, the night both women were attacked?"

"I went to a Halloween party until around 11 or so, and then I came home and crashed. I was supposed to work the next day."

"And your brother was at his friend's house?"

"Yeah," Alex threw up his hands in surrender, "after the party I've got no alibi. But I gave a blood test at the station and that will clear me. I was here."

"Do you have any idea who could have done this?"

"No. Everyone liked Melissa. Even as a food inspector, she had a reputation for being easygoing. Someone really needed to mess up bad for her to report them. Melissa didn't have enemies. No one wanted to hurt her." Tears broke and rolled down his sunken cheeks. "I'm done, I think. Can we be done?"

"No problem man," Jack said before I could respond. "Camera's off."

"We're good," I agreed, frustrated that Jack had stepped on my toes and made the call before I was finished. At this point, the interview's flow had been interrupted and I was pretty sure I'd gotten enough, so I let it go. "Thank you, Alex."

I reached over and rested my hand on his trembling shoulder. He looked lost. "I'm very sorry for your loss." I wished I had something better to say. I also wondered if he would ever realize what a great girl he had missed out on. Melissa deserved more than Alex was ready to give her.

While Jack broke down the tripod and gathered interior shots, I typed in my phone and posted updates on Twitter and Instagram about our exclusive interview with Melissa Rossi's ex-boyfriend.

Saying our goodbyes and walking out the door, I thought it seemed pretty obvious Alex was innocent. "What do you think? Did you believe him?" I asked Jack as he prepared to take some exterior shots of the home.

"It felt like his vibe was pretty legit. I feel bad for the guy. He'll always have to carry what happened to those girls with him." Jack clicked opened the news car's passenger door for me so I could sit and review my notes.

"So, what are you doing tonight?" he asked before he went to gather the final footage for our story.

Letting out a deep breath, I rubbed my fingers on my temples. "I guess everyone's meeting up at *The Point* for drinks."

"Should be chill."

"Totally," I said, only half-way paying attention. My mind was drifting back to that threatening note. Would today's interview make things worse?

I honestly didn't feel like hanging out with any of my coworkers besides Jack. But going out sounded a whole lot better than hibernating alone in my apartment worrying about a potential stalker and thinking about dead girls.

CHAPTER FOUR

The staccato beat of a drum tapped out melodic vibrations above a sea of voices floating out to *The Point's* small parking lot. I stubbed my cigarette on the retainer wall and chucked my bottle of beer into a recycling bin. Our weekend anchor, Lily, shivered in the cool night air with Kaya and me. Jack slid off his black jacket and offered it my way. When I declined, Kaya accepted it without hesitation.

I tried not to show my jealousy at the way she looked at him with her big moon eyes, but my mood had shifted into a state of supreme aggravation. In addition to finding that note, an anonymous viewer had called the station minutes before I left work.

Jack, as usual, noticed. "Shelbs, what's bothering you?"

I shifted the weight on my hips and attempted to appear nonchalant. "It's nothing, really."

"Nothing?" Kaya laughed, "You've got some tea. Spill it."

Feeling uncomfortable sharing, but wanting to vent, my hands clenched into fists. "Travis told me some dumb guy called in and said I was too nice to Melissa Rossi's ex-boyfriend today in my interview. The caller suggested a real reporter, like that badass Keisha Grant over at Channel 7, should be covering our lead story. He also said my eyebrows were too thin and that I look really ugly in red lipstick." Travis had chuckled when he relayed the obnoxious message to me, but that was the least of what rattled me. It was difficult not to wonder if the caller wasn't the same person who had left me the note. Was the stalker calling my work, too?

"That's bull." Kaya took another pull on her beer. "How many times a month do we get a call like that? And it's never about the male reporters, only the women."

"Who cares what any of us look like? My eyebrows are amazing, just like my reporting skills." I flicked my hair and tried to keep calm. "Should we go in? We can text Travis to meet up with us inside."

Headlights cut through the packed parking lot, momentarily blinding us before our sports anchor's SUV wedged into the last remaining space.

"He's here." Lily cast her shiny black hair over her slim shoulder and nodded with smugness. It was her idea to pregame while we waited for Travis to wrap up his nightshift.

I'd almost begged Jack to change plans with me when I heard Lily was coming. At least once a week, after the rest of the crew took off for the night, Lily would bribe the director and one of the production assistants with donuts and pizza to stay late and record her while she reread the evening's news stories at the anchor desk, pretending she was live on air.

Lily wanted every word she spoke, all of her gestures and inflections, to be polished and perfect for her anchor résumé reel. If she flubbed a word, she started over from scratch. She was passing off a staged performance to potential employers as if it were a real show where she only had one chance to get it right.

It was cheating. But Lily didn't care about that, she was determined to make it to a big market faster than any of us. Her fake Colgate smile and relentless drive exacerbated my competitive side and worked my last nerve.

Travis exited his silver Infinity and strode in our direction with a cool confidence. "Hey." He lifted his chin as a hello. "Looks like I'm right on time." I watched him sniff at my lingering cigarette smoke, unconsciously smoothing out his dirty-blond hair.

"Ready to meet some ladies?" I smirked at Travis.

"I'm down."

From the corner of my eyes, I caught the subtle relaxing of Lily's ear-to-ear smile.

"Let's do this." Jack rubbed his hands together. "It's getting cold out here."

Stepping inside, I scanned the sleek interior of our regular haunt. A pool table, large flat-screen high definition televisions, and a long, stained concrete bar with a high gloss finish greeted us. Liquor lined the narrow shelves behind the bar, featuring twenty taps of different Oregon craft beers.

The live music in the back corner consisted of an enthusiastic drummer, a skinny guitar player, and a scruffy tambourine-tapping guy who missed the memo about tambourine's being out of style. The place reeked of stale beer and patchouli oil.

"Let's grab a place to sit." Travis's long athletic body broke free of our pack and led the way to a large, wooden high-bar table. "I've got the first round." He reached for a seat and the rest of us followed suit.

Within minutes, our bubbly cocktail waitress, dressed in all black, came around with a towel. She wiped at the water beading on the table and smiled hello to all of us before pulling out her notepad and taking Travis' order. Along with pitchers of beer, he asked for *The Point's* famous marionberry candied hazelnuts.

"I love this band." Kaya bobbed her innocent round face to the beat.

"You know these guys?" Jack asked her over the din of the music.

"Yeah, I go to SOU with one of them. They're called *My Father Likes a Man in Uniform*. Isn't that awesome?" She laughed.

I envied Kaya's carefree spirit. She wasn't like the rest of us. She'd grown up in this charming small town with her loving, all-American, intact family.

Her brother and sister had probably come with her parents to cheer her on when she played high school softball. I could imagine Kaya taking annual summer camping trips with her family and gathering in the living room each Christmas to eat popcorn and watch their favorite old movies. Her life seemed so intoxicatingly normal.

Jack tapped his hands on the table from the seat next to mine. "They have a nice vibe. It actually reminds me of a band I grew up with back home."

"That's so cool." Kaya, who'd already knocked back a couple of drinks in the parking lot, reached out and touched Jack's face like they were a couple, running the tip of her index finger down the line of his scar. "How'd you get this sexy scar?"

Jealousy gripped me hard. I wanted to snatch her hand off him.

"I took a fin to the mouth."

"Oh my gosh," she said, touching her lips. "What does that even mean?"

He leaned forward with enthusiasm. "It happened when I was out at Pacific Beach one day, by Crystal Pier. The waves weren't too big, the water was clean. Nice little tubes. I pulled into one and tried to pump inside to get some speed and I caught a rail. My board went up and over, and I tumbled. While I was under water something hit me in the mouth."

"Ouch." She looked at him with her saucer eyes.

"I thought it was no big deal, just the rail bumping into me, so I grabbed my board and started to paddle back out. That's when I looked down and saw the blood. I tried to close my mouth and it wouldn't shut all the way."

"Oh no." She covered her own mouth as if it had happened to her.

"Hole in my chin that I could stick my finger through into my mouth. Lost a tooth, had a fractured jaw. Left this gnarly scar."

"I like it." She kept her blue eyes fixed on his. "Makes you look rugged, like, more of a man."

My whole body tensed with irrational anger. Even though I refused to be anything more than friends with Jack, I still wanted him. Kaya and I weren't buddies. She didn't owe me anything. But she was totally coming on to Jack, and it seemed like Jack was encouraging her.

"I guess it's a better story than tripping over a rake," I said, burning with heated sarcasm.

Jack went silent while Kaya looked at me with confusion. Covering those gruesome murders followed by a threatening note on my door and then a suspicious call to my work, had left me feeling cornered and vulnerable, and the alcohol wasn't helping. The toxic combination made me mean.

Before I could apologize, Lily stepped in and questioned Jack. "Why'd you ever leave San Diego? Weren't you a big-time surfer there?" It was a subject Jack had avoided discussing with any of us—even me. Lily knew it was off-limits.

"That's in the past." Jack clenched his jaw.

Our waitress set down two pitchers of golden ale and a bunch of chilled glasses for us to pass around.

"Didn't you move up here only a year and a half ago?" she asked, going into reporter mode, poking around harder.

"It's been two years," he said.

"That's not very long ago. Did you already forget why you left?" She took a sip of beer.

"Stop." I glowered at Lily. It was one thing for me to give Jack a hard time. We were close. I cared about him. Lily was just being rude.

"What?" Lily smiled with a fake innocence. "Everyone knows Jack's guarding some deep dark mystery from his past. We all want to know what made him give up his favorite sport and leave his hometown."

Jack stared back at Lily. "It's over."

"Why?" Lily asked, setting down her glass.

"It's none of your business, Lily," I said. "You don't need to interrogate him."

"Excuse me." Jack stood up.

As I watched him storm toward the bar, I debated whether or not to join him.

Before I could make a move, I caught Lily rolling her eyes in disrespect. "What's his problem?"

My fingers curled around the hazelnuts in my hand, cracking them in my grasp. "What's *your* problem Lily?"

Her perfectly made-up lips formed a sneer. "I don't know. Why don't you tell me, Shelby? You're the *NBC 4* lead investigative reporter."

I glared at Lily, warning her to drop it.

"Who wants to do a shot with me?" Travis laced his hands around his beer glass, changing the conversation back to himself.

Lily laughed. "Great idea."

"I'm ready for a Big O." Travis smirked at her. "Wanna join me?"

Lily nodded.

"What'll it be?" he asked Lily, motioning to our waitress.

Lily giggled. "How about a Blow Job."

"Anyone else?" He raised an eyebrow at Kaya and me.

"Ta-kill-ya." Kaya bobbed her head in excitement. "Shots, shots, shots!"

"Shelbs?" Travis held eye contact with me.

"I'll take a double vodka cranberry."

He let out a bark of laughter before he spoke. "Hardcore."

"It's a warmup." I said, scanning the crowd, searching for Jack. I eventually found him turning away from the bar, looking in our direction as if he could feel me watching. He strolled back to our table, another pint of beer in hand.

After killing the last rounds from the pitcher while we waited for our shots, I switched topics to something less controversial, like work. "Have any of you guys heard anything new about the murders on Belle Street?"

In the past couple of hours, social media had all but

confirmed the identity of the second victim. It was indeed the beauty queen: Daphne DeLuca, age twenty-three, born and raised in small town, Centre, Alabama.

I'd stalked her makeup account on Instagram. Raven haired with big green eyes and high cheekbones, she was every bit as beautiful as in her pictures. With one hundred thousand followers in a small town like Ashland, she wasn't the kind of girl who lived under the radar.

In other breaking news, Melissa Rossi's supposed best friend had called the station this afternoon. To avoid the typical newsroom eavesdroppers who would happily steal a lead, I'd walked outside the building and called her back on my cell.

She wanted to make a plea to the public to find her friend's killer. She and her fiancé, who also hung out with Melissa, were going to meet me at Lithia Park first thing tomorrow morning for an interview. Despite any concerns regarding my personal safety, I was going to get another exclusive, my third in a row, a major coup in the news business.

Scanning my coworkers faces, I was eager for more details before I met with the best friend. When no one spoke, I offered them some information. Tit for tat. "I heard the third roommate, the only one who survived, fled to her parents' home up in Portland. I guess she didn't feel safe living alone in Ashland with a killer on the loose."

"What if she is the killer?" Jack asked.

I tapped my fingers on the table. "The police are probably waiting on DNA samples before ruling her out as a suspect. In the meantime, what're they gonna do?" I looked over my colleagues once again. "None of you've heard anything else?" They had to know something. We were journalists, information was our currency.

Kaya's eyes lit up. "Some of my friends at school said the murdered women sold Molly. Maybe they owed someone money."

Lily shook back her black hair and looked directly at Travis as she spoke to me. "Some people are saying it was a mafia hit. You know, because both the victims had Italian last names. DeLuca and Rossi."

"Nah." Travis shook his head. "Just because your last name's Italian doesn't mean the mob's after you. That whole mafia story seems made up."

Lily touched Travis's hand. "Let's order more drinks."

Kaya, glancing over at Jack, fiddled with her pendant necklace engraved with the word #Cute. "It could have been prostitution. Melissa Rossi might've been pimping her roommate out." Kaya pulled her focus away from Jack and frowned at me. "Don't roll your eyes, Shelby. There's a lot of money in sex. Do you know how many girls strip to pay their student loans? A real-life Ms. Alabama could have stacks on stacks of cash."

"Ms. Greater Gadsden," I corrected Kaya. "She didn't take state. But, I guess." I ran my tongue across my top teeth. "I still think the killer's a vengeful ex, whether it was some guy Daphne DeLuca had dated or someone from Melissa Rossi's past."

"Sad." Kaya snuck another peek at Jack. "Sucks those women even had to deal with such jerks."

"You're changing the subject," I countered. "Besides, not everyone's looking for a relationship. Sometimes a woman just wants a hook-up; easy in, easy out."

"Even still, why wouldn't you be with someone who treats you right?"

Because you could fall hopelessly in love with a good man. I felt myself flushing, articulating my issues out loud would only tempt fate. Romantic love was something I'd spent a lifetime avoiding, and now it was more important than ever. Love could sidetrack a budding career, throw you so far off you never fully recovered.

I saw what it did to my dad. Love left him needy and broken. It did even worse things to my mom. "Never mind," I said to Kaya, wiping the hazelnuts off my hands and standing up. "I'm going to play pool."

Travis nearly jumped from his chair to join me. "I'll play you. I gotta warn you though, I'm really good. You'll be rackin' my balls all night." He gawked at me with a sloppy smirk. "No strings attached."

I shot him a dirty look. He was an idiot if he thought he was a candidate for me even breathing in his general direction.

Across the room, I picked up one of the smaller cue sticks and sized up the recently vacated pool table.

"You know the rules?" Travis asked with a smug curiosity, his faint East Coast prep-school accent swimming in my ears.

"Why, you think you can be a big man and teach me?" I snagged the triangle and racked the balls. Travis had no idea who he was dealing with.

Rubbing the tip of my cue in colored chalk, I placed the white ball in position. Travis grabbed his own cue stick and leaned forward into my personal space, watching. I knew plenty of guys like Travis, guys who liked to dominate their environment. Spreading my feet a little, I grasped the base of the stick with my left hand and rested the narrow end on my right hand.

"You're a lefty." Travis licked his bottom lip.

"Very observant," I murmured.

I practiced my stroke, my eyes switching from the contact point on the cue ball to the spot I was aiming for on the yellow object ball. I made my shot. The white ball broke the rack and two stripes sunk into the pockets.

Travis's eyebrows lifted in surprise. "Not bad."

"Let's see if you even get a chance to shoot."

Ten minutes later I declared myself victorious. Travis grabbed our beers and we continued playing for more than an hour. I won three out of four.

The thrill of taking him down and the large quantity of alcohol coursing through my one-hundred-and-ten-pound body swirled into a euphoria. "Champion." I fist pumped the air. "You can suck it, Travis."

He grimaced at me in response, which only made me happier. The room began to spin. I felt my arms and legs tingle. Before I could stop myself, I found my arms encircling his neck in a triumphant hug. "Winner," I taunted into his ear.

His lips found mine. Travis kissed me with an aggressive urgency and I stupidly pressed in for more. I wanted to cross lines, obliterate any of my aggravating problems. It was a brief moment of abandon until I opened my eyes and spotted the true object of my affection sitting at the table watching.

I caught the look of hurt in Jack's eyes before he recovered. Placing a casual arm around Kaya, Jack used his free hand to chug his beer.

My heart pulsed in my neck. I closed my lips and shoved my hand against Travis's chest. "Cut it out, it was just a hug."

"Great game," he leered.

"Don't be a dick."

"I thought you liked jerks. We're easy marks."

Ignoring him, I stumbled back over to our table and dragged out a chair. Lily scowled into her empty glass as Travis placed his hand on the back of my seat like he owned me. He nudged my chair in and squeezed himself into the seat between Lily and me, clearly eager for more action.

"I'm over it." Jack slammed his glass on the table. "I'm outta here."

"You Ubering?" Kaya's fingers touched the rim of Jack's empty cup.

"Nah, it's a beautiful night. I'm gonna walk."

"Oh." Her lower lip protruded in a pout.

His arm still draped around her shoulder, Jack hugged Kaya to his side. "You live close by. Want me to walk you home?"

She nodded and the two of them said their goodbyes before exiting the bar together, leaving me alone to stew and come up with a new plan of my own for the evening.

CHAPTER FIVE

Having said my own sloppy goodbyes and cursing out Jack under my breath for taking off with Kaya, I stumbled across Main Street feeling completely paranoid. I lit a cigarette and looked over my shoulder for any creepers as I passed the neon restaurant signs and sidestepped handfuls of dreadlocked homeless hippies smoking weed and playing music for money.

When I reached the black and white striped awning over *Algernon's Creole*, I leaned up against the wall and took a few more drags, scanning the boulevard for stalkers. *Quit acting like a fool, Shelby.*

I told myself I had nothing to fear. One dumb little note left by a coward meant nothing. People called into the station all the time with complaints. It didn't mean there was any connection to the note.

Stubbing out my cigarette against my shoe, I tossed the butt in a garbage can. The French Quarter-style restaurant featured a rooftop bar that catered to the affluent San Francisco tourists who filled our town from June through mid-October during the Shakespeare Festival. It was one of my top hangouts for a very specific reason.

Climbing narrow backstairs, I headed straight for the dimly lit bar, hoping to find the main attraction back at work. To my delight, I spotted Julien, the super hot bartender, popping open a bottle of red wine. "Hey, stranger." I waved to my second favorite guy in town, a French import with stunning sea-green eyes and a deeply cleft chin.

"Shelby, good to see you. The usual?" he asked. My troubles eased at the sound of his thick accent.

"Vodka shot." I leaned toward the bar. "I'm going to take it over to a table."

He handed me a bowl of blanched almonds. "This is serious." He chuckled. "Take a seat wherever you like, I will be over soon."

Five or ten minutes later, Julien sauntered toward my table for two, tucked in the corner by the front street-facing window. "I brought you something different, a glass of Crianza. On me."

"Thanks." I swirled the wine in its glass and took a sniff. Mixing alcohols was probably going to make me puke. Then again, every move I'd made tonight was stupid, why stop now? "It smells delicious."

"It tastes even better." He nodded. "What brings you in here? We're getting ready to close."

"I wanted a last drink before I walked home."

"That's kind of a far walk, no? Especially after what happened." His voice dropped, heavy with sorrow.

The murders on Belle Street must have gotten to him too. All of Ashland was on edge. It was as if, in the dark shadows of the night, death had crawled its way into those girls' home at random, and he could've picked anybody.

Any one of us could be next.

Looking closer at Julien, I noticed his eyes were swollen, the whites, pink. Considering how intoxicated I was, they had to be pretty bad for me to notice. "You don't look so good." I tilted my head in concern, careful not to slur my words. "You haven't been around the past few months."

He rubbed at his nose. "I took some time off here and there, but I've been around. You must have come in on the nights I was off."

"What's up?" I asked, rubbing my eyes for clarity, certain something was troubling him.

He dragged his hand down his stubbled face, over his mouth, passed his cleft chin. "It's been a rough few days. Working is good. It keeps my mind clear. Listen, I will drive you home. It's not safe out there. Hang out for about thirty minutes or so?"

Julien was naturally cautious. He'd worked for the French police department in riot and SWAT for nearly a decade. Then he traveled to the Central African Republic to serve as a UN peacekeeper. He was the toughest guy I knew. The kind of man who made you feel safe at night.

"You're worth the wait." I held his gaze with a loopy grin as I sipped my wine. With Jack off doing who knew what with Kaya, I had no intention of going home alone.

———

Julien turned his black pick-up truck off the quiet tree-lined street and pulled into the immaculate alley fronting my rental unit. I lived in a pretty two-bedroom, two-bath, cheerful yellow apartment built over the detached garage of a gorgeous estate home. It was significantly more luxurious than the run-down places most of my colleagues rented closer to the news station, but my obscenely wealthy parents had insisted I live somewhere nice. Anything low-rent scared them.

As usual, they ignored my protests about wanting to fit in, and to keep them off my back, I put a deposit on this place. Refusing to take a dime of their money, I paid the rent with cash I'd made selling off several pieces of jewelry Dad had gifted me over the years. I was currently bleeding out all my savings from the part-jobs I'd worked in college. Paychecks at small town news stations were a joke.

Julien left the engine running. "Here you are."

"Thanks." I smiled, breathing in his seductive woodsy caramel scent, waiting for him to make a move. Julien had separated from his wife more than a year ago and, shortly after I moved here, we'd hooked up a couple of times.

Julien looked straight ahead, his hands gripping the steering wheel. "Be safe tonight, okay? I'll watch you walk in."

"Sure." I wasn't ready to leave. "Hey, I wanted to ask you, I've got an interview in the morning with Melissa Rossi's best friend. Melissa is one of the girls who was murdered on Belle Street."

He inspected his fingernails. "I know who she is."

"The best friend's name is Liberty. She's kinda pushy. I was wondering, do you know her? Have you heard anything about her?" My eyes had trouble focusing. Carrying on a conversation without slurring my words was becoming increasingly challenging.

"It's a small town," he said, turning down the temperature

on his truck's heater.

"You've seen her at your bar?" I leaned in a little closer to him, trying to sound sober.

He twisted the thick silver ring on his left index finger and continued to avoid making eye contact. "Liberty came around a few times with Melissa and her friends."

"What do you know about her?"

"Not much."

"Did they ever come in with the other woman who died, Daphne Deluca, the beauty queen?"

Julien finally looked up at me in surprise. "I didn't know they identified the other woman who was killed."

"It's not official, but you know, nothing stays secret for long. So, did you ever see any of them?"

"The girls came in sometimes in a big group. They seemed a little harsh on Daphne, you know?"

"They were mean to her?"

"No. They just seemed..." His voice trailed off. "She was a gorgeous girl. I could tell the other women were envious of all the attention men gave her. Especially Liberty."

I ran my hand through my hair, running a loose brown strand around my index finger, smiling at Julien. "How so?"

"I don't know, they would roll their eyes, or Liberty would get louder and try to get attention back to her. It made me feel bad for Daphne. She wasn't trying to stand out. She couldn't help it."

"Yeah ... hey, why don't you park and come in?" I was too wasted to concentrate any longer and was ready to move the action indoors.

"That's okay."

"Why not?" I leaned in closer. My hands reached up his

back and through his soft cropped hair. Julien offered the perfect distraction from Jack, the murders, that frightening note. Whatever was bothering him, he could forget about it, too.

"Shelby." He pulled away from me, his voice thick with emotion. "You're a beautiful girl, but I can't do this."

Confused and hurt, I drew back as well. "Are you getting back together with your wife?"

"No."

"Are you afraid you'll get caught with me? Could it mess up your divorce settlement?"

"I have nothing for her to take. Besides, I don't have anything to hide. I told her months ago there's no chance to reconcile. We're finished for certain."

"Oh." My head felt dizzy.

"Look, I wanted to make sure you got home safe. You're a friend."

A friend. I wanted out of the car. Immediately. "Thanks for the ride Julien." Humiliated, I gathered up my purse and jacket and yanked open the door.

"Don't take it personally, Shelby. I just can't do this tonight."

I waved my hand as I shut the door. "Goodbye, Julien. *Don't* call me."

———

Sometime later, after I'd heaved into my resentful toilet at least a dozen times, the doorbell rang. Julien must have reconsidered. Practicing the words I would use to reject him, I guided myself in the dark. With wobbly hands, I grappled pristine white walls down the long stairway from the main floor of my apartment to the entryway.

"Hey," I said, flipping on the porch light. Before opening the door, I warned him, "If you're back for a second chance, you can forget it."

No response. I held the handle of the closed door.

"Hello?" I said from the shelter of my darkened entryway. Goosebumps formed on my arms and the back of my neck.

Silence.

Still drunk, but becoming increasingly alert, my heart began to slam in my chest. I took a deep breath and counted to five. "Julien?"

Nothing. I cursed the homeowners for not putting in a peep hole. *Was Julien messing with me?*

Pressing my ear to the door and listening, I girded myself for a fight and ripped opened the door. No Julien. No anybody.

Instead, I found a new note taped to the outside.

I ripped it off the door and slammed it shut, twisting the lock tight. With trembling hands, I unfolded the computer paper.

Hello Ms. Day, get a clue, take one step closer and the Belle Street Killer will come after YOU.

CHAPTER SIX

Great holes of deep blue sky punctured fluffy white clouds. Dew drops from an overnight rain clung to the Japanese maples and dogwood trees sheltering the lower duck pond at Lithia Park. My entire body began to shake when I read that second note in the middle of the night.

My instincts told me to run. I was in danger. No story was worth sticking around for, especially so far away from the safety of home.

But I reminded myself how hard I'd fought to get here, how important is was to be a success at something that mattered. All my life, teachers, friends, even relatives, brushed me off as a spoiled little rich girl. No matter how hard I worked—impeccable grades, first place awards in figure skating competitions, perfect behavior—no one took me seriously. All that mattered to them was my parents' bank account.

This was my opportunity to prove myself, to show I was not only a strong and independent woman, but that I could do anything in this world I put my mind to. I'd landed a career-defining opportunity. If I gave up because of one creep, I'd lose my momentum. I'd end up wasting my chance.

Besides, those notes could be nothing more than some impotent stranger trying to scare me. And if I told the police or reported them directly to my boss, the news station might begin to view me as a liability and pull me off real reporting. For all I knew, it was one of my coworkers trying to steal my lead story.

My cousin had told me about a general assignment reporter at her LA news station who was fired after he got caught trying to bribe his assignment editor with season tickets to the Lakers in exchange for letting him cover the entertainment beat on Oscar night. Television reporters could be cutthroat. It was wise to stay alert and watch your back.

I took a deep breath and steadied my pounding head. Last night's partying was still kicking my butt. Luckily, Melissa Rossi's best friend had suggested the perfect spot for our morning's interview. Colorful autumn leaves and outdoor greenery would make an appealing background.

Joggers passed me by as I straightened the legs on the tripod right off the paved trail and set up my camera. I checked my phone for the third time. 9:30 a.m. Liberty was running thirty minutes late. She was going to throw off my entire day's schedule if she didn't hurry up.

"Shelby?" A woman's voice sung out my name.

I whipped around expecting to find Liberty. Instead I saw Kaya, with her unrelenting joy, strolling straight toward me. I tried to keep my face friendly.

"Good morning." Carrying her own set of camera equipment, Kaya smiled even wider. With her chipper demeanor, as sweet as a cookies-and-cream cupcake, she really ought to have considered angling to become a weather girl rather than a serious journalist.

"What are you doing here so early?" she asked.

"I've got an interview with someone about the murders on Belle Street."

Kaya stopped in front of me and lifted her sunglasses onto her head. "You get the best stories."

I'd earned it. "What about you? Why are you here?"

Our news director had convinced Kaya to take the weekend assignment editor position. It was a thankless job nobody really wanted, but in this business, everybody had to pay their dues. We all took on work around the newsroom we didn't love in order to move up through the ranks. As an attractive, educated local girl doing her time on the weekend assignment desk, Kaya had a genuine shot of getting promoted to on-air reporting, one of the most coveted jobs in the newsroom.

"Carolyn asked me if I wanted to come in early to get some footage and write up something on the dead ducks people have been finding here."

"That's cool she gave you a story to practice on," I said with sincerity. Despite the way she'd made off with Jack last night, Kaya deserved the chance to hone her reporting skills.

Kaya pursed her glossy pink lips. Making her best sad face she said, "Yeah. Someone reported seeing some kids throwing rocks in the park. They think that might be what's killing the ducks."

"Poor birds." I shielded my dehydrated, burning eyes from the emerging sunshine.

Kaya pushed her sunglasses back down onto her face.

"Hey, so I wanted to ask you about last night. You looked a
little upset. You and Jack aren't a thing? Because I wouldn't—"

"Don't worry about it. I'm not looking for a boyfriend.
I came to Ashland to work." It was the truth, even if I did
find myself aching for more. My stomach lurched, the
sickening combination of a hangover, anxiety, and longing
for something I couldn't have.

"So it's cool if Jack and I are friends. Right?"

Thankfully, a shaggy-haired blond guy, sporting a
black "Made in Oregon" sweatshirt, cut into our awkward
conversation.

"Sorry, we're late," he said, rubbing the shoulders of
someone I could only suspect was Liberty, a schlumpy girl
with long, wavy brown hair. "Lib needed a bit of time to
breathe before going out. It's been hard."

Kaya gave Liberty a pitiful smile and turned to me.
"Okay, I'm outta here. See you later, alligator."

I said goodbye to Kaya and shook Liberty's hand. Tears
immediately began to fall down her face, carving valleys
through her spotty foundation.

"I'm so sorry for your loss, Liberty. Thank you for
coming today."

"Thank you." She swiped at her wet cheeks. "I can't
believe it's real."

I looked up to her fiancé, who stood behind her, rubbing
Liberty's shoulders.

"Maybe you can stand with her during the interview," I
said.

He shrugged, his eyes darting down to Liberty's
trembling shoulders.

She sucked in her bottom lip and smoothed out her

long-sleeved yellow blouse. "I can do it. I won't let that man get to me. Brandon's kinda shy, anyway."

"You've got this, Lib." Brandon wrapped his arms around his fiancé's torso, giving her a reassuring kiss on the top of her head. She put on a brave face and wiped away her tears. Seeing her fiancé's warm, comforting embrace reminded me of the way Jack hugged Kaya close last night. It made me want to reconsider my romance goals.

Brandon came and stood beside me, pulling a pack of cigarettes from the pocket of his hooded sweatshirt. I wouldn't have pegged him as a smoker. "Where's your cameraman? You all alone?" he asked.

"We only get help if we're going live, or if it's a real slow news day and we've got extra hands on board. Mostly I'm a one-man-band at *NBC 4 News*; the reporter, photographer, and the video editor."

"I see." He rolled a cigarette in between his fingers, staring at the camera facing his fiancé. "Do you mind if I smoke?"

"No problem." I waved him off and started setting up the camera.

He must've noticed me sneaking a glance as he lit up, because he held out his pack to me. Camel Turkish Gold. It wasn't my usual brand, but I could feel the satisfaction in my mouth.

The addict in me wanted to rip the cigarette out of his hand. "No, thanks." I licked my tongue across my lower lip and bit it. Smoking at work was unprofessional, there was no way I would do anything to risk losing this story.

"I'm ready when you are." I turned to Liberty. "Do you want to take a moment, or should we get started?"

She dug out a tissue from her purse and dabbed it on her running eyeliner. Crumpling it in her hand, she squeezed the limp Kleenex for security. "I'm ready." She handed the purse to her fiancé. "Let's just get this done. It's important for Melissa."

"You're doing the right thing." I kicked at the dirt. "Honestly, I admire your courage. I can't even think about how it would feel to lose your best friend."

I thought about my friends back home, very much alive. We had gotten into trouble in high school, I even dropped out my junior year to spend more time with them. But I knew what I wanted in life, and I needed to graduate. After several months of running wild, I earned my GED, enrolled in college, and, no surprise, we grew apart. I missed them, especially whenever I saw them all having fun and going out on their Instagram or Snapchat Stories.

Still, even though we'd built different lives, I knew I could count on my ride-or-die friends if I needed them. Liberty would never have this.

I realized as I eyed the silver engagement ring on her finger, she'd lost her maid of honor too. Melissa would never stand next to Liberty and Brandon on their wedding day, holding the bouquet, and giving a silly speech about all the inside jokes and funny stories they'd shared.

I shuffled behind the camera, hit the power button and held out a shotgun microphone. "Testing, testing, testing," I spoke out loud, making sure the sound worked. "Okay, Liberty, you can stand there and look over at me. Try to ignore the camera and pretend like it's just the two of us talking. I need you to say and spell your last name and tell me how you knew Melissa."

Once I had her information on tape and the camera in proper focus, we got started. "Liberty, how did you meet Melissa?"

She sniffled and tucked her hair behind her ears before speaking. "Melissa and I grew up together in Chiloquin. We've been best friends since the fifth grade. I even picked the same college so we could be together." Liberty's face crumpled. Fresh tears fell, but she continued. "I would've been her roommate if I'd moved into that house with her on Belle Street like we'd planned. But I got fired from my job for coming in late, and it took me months to find something else. By then, Melissa was already settled in. We still saw each other almost every day, though."

"She must've talked to you about her boyfriend, Alex Haskell?"

"Melissa would talk to me about everything. I didn't like Alex, he was a jerk and seemed to make her more sad than happy. It got to the point where I'd lose track of which days they were together or not. It's like they split up so much, she was embarrassed to talk about him, so she stopped telling me what was going on."

"And what about the other guy Melissa had started dating?"

Liberty smirked. "There was no other guy. Melissa made him up to make Alex jealous. Of course, it didn't do any good. Alex didn't care."

Red and yellow leaves fluttered in the cool breeze as the rising sun peeked out from the clouds. I squinted my eyes, holding my focus on Liberty. "Alex seemed like a good guy when I interviewed him. Do you think he could've actually hurt Melissa?"

"He puts on a good show, but he has a temper and can be a real douche. Alex gave Melissa a hard time about a few extra pounds she'd put on. He told her she'd embarrassed him the last time she pigged out in front of his friends. Who says something like that?! It's like all he cares about is his stupid image."

"Wow." I hadn't gotten that vibe from him at all. "That sucks," I said, breathing in the tempting scent of cigarette smoke.

Melissa looked over at her fiancé. "Brandon, didn't you tell me Alex complained to you about Melissa?"

Brandon took a drag on his cigarette. "Alex said she could be kind of a stalker. He said he'd gone out one night when he and Melissa where on a break and she showed up out of nowhere. Alex'd been talking to some cute SOU girl and Melissa kind of got in the way. He seemed pretty pissed. I don't know though." Brandon shrugged. "Most of the time, he was cool."

I looked back at Liberty. "Besides not getting along with Alex, did Melissa have any enemies that you know of? Were there any restaurant owners mad at her for giving them a bad rating?"

"No, she would've told me. I don't think this could've had anything to do with Melissa. Her roommate, Daphne, was hooking up with every random guy she could find. She didn't want to go to their places, so she kept sneaking them home at night. You don't know what can happen when you mess around like that. It wasn't safe, and I'd told Melissa that." Liberty wrapped her arms around her chest. "Right, babe?" she asked Brandon.

"I only wish we'd invited her over for Halloween." Brandon

drew on his cigarette with force until it glowed brightly, then he flicked it away and exhaled the smoke.

"How have you been holding up, Liberty?" I asked.

"It hurts to breathe. It's like someone took a baseball bat and slammed it into my stomach as hard as they could. Most of the time I don't even want to move."

I held my silence.

"I want to scream at the sky. I don't know why this happened. I don't know why it was her. She was the best person in the world, nobody would want to hurt her. I've never felt so horrible. I don't know what to do without her." She dabbed a tissue against her swollen eyes, her shoulders racking in pain.

"I'm so sorry." I held my breath for composure, not knowing what to say that would bring her comfort. "Is there anything you want people to know about Melissa?"

"She was my best friend. She was like my sister. Her mom and dad and brothers are great people and they all need her. Melissa worked so hard to get through school and she loved being a health inspector. She loved her friends too, and she wanted to travel the world. Melissa fought hard to have such a great life, and somebody stole that from her. Someone stole her from all of us." Tears slipped down her red cheeks.

"Is there anything you want to say to people watching this story who may know more about this?"

"Yes." She looked at Brandon. He nodded back at her, his presence seeming to encourage her to speak up. "I want to say to everyone watching, someone out there seeing this has to have seen something that's not right. Ashland isn't as close-knit as where Melissa and I grew up, but it's a place where the locals know each other and look out for each other. You can't—" Melissa bit her lip before taking a shaky breath, "You can't murder two girls and walk away like nothing's happened. Please, if you know anything, please, *please* call the police."

I cleared my throat and prepared to ask her the question I always saved for last. During an internship in a West Hollywood newsroom, a seasoned reporter had taught me to ask this vague question, because nearly every time, it elicited the best responses during an interview. "Liberty. What's the bottom line?"

She looked slightly confused. As she lowered her brows in thought, her face quivered with sorrow. "Melissa's mom had to look at her body. The police say Melissa was hurt defending herself, she had bruises and cuts on her hands. Melissa fought back hard. Whoever did this has to be hurt, too, or acting weird somehow." Liberty stared into the dark lens of my recording camera. "Please help Melissa. Daphne too. They didn't deserve this. We are hurt so badly. Not knowing who did this, having to wonder if every person we talk to is the one. It makes everything worse. We don't want to have to think about it anymore. We want to bury our friends in peace."

Liberty shuddered as I powered off the camera. Brandon took the finishing drag on his second cigarette, flicked it to the ground and reached out to hold Liberty as she collapsed into his arms.

CHAPTER SEVEN

A flock of blackbirds soared in the dust-gray sky that late Saturday afternoon. Eight days after the murders, I drove alone, climbing in elevation through dense forests and towering ridgelines of the Cascade Mountain Range, heading toward the tiny town of Chiloquin. Liberty had asked me to attend Melissa Rossi's funeral. Melissa's parents had also given their consent.

After watching my coverage of their daughter's murder, her parents trusted me. We all agreed that as painful as it was to have media at such a sacred commemoration, it was an important opportunity to gather information as well as keep the crime front and center in the public eye.

Wiping at my sleepless eyes, I snaked along the seventy-eight miles of gasping autumn colors. Sharp pine needles grew thick on tall evergreens. The ice blue sky opened up before me in an endless expanse. I'd never felt so alone.

What if the stress of the past few days overwhelmed me and I went into a full-blown panic attack behind the wheel? What if I got a flat tire and my stalker came out of nowhere to run me over? I knew it was ridiculous, but now, more than ever, I craved the comfort of congested boulevards throbbing with energy, the smell of exhaust, and densely populated living. High decibel sirens and irate drivers equaled safety in numbers.

My cell, resting on my lap, rang, and I checked the caller ID. Jack hadn't spoken a friendly word to me all week. He was acting as if we'd been in an actual romantic relationship and I'd cheated on him. At least I knew he was avoiding me because he cared. My resolve to make it on my own, no strings attached, was weakening, and parts of me wanted him more than ever.

Sure enough, it wasn't Jack on the line. Disappointed, I slipped my index finger across the screen to answer. "Hello?"

"*Privet solnishko. Kak ti?*" Mom greeted me in Russian. I pictured her beautiful face pressed against her phone as she raced around running errands. Mom, with all her OCD anxiety, rarely sat still.

"*Horosho*, Mama," I said before switching to English. "I was just thinking about you. What's up?"

"You must've been missing me. I was calling to check on you. How's it going becoming a superstar investigative reporter?" The taint of sarcasm seeped from her tongue.

Mom resented my move. This dream job belonged to my father and me. As far as she saw it, her only daughter had abandoned her. Forget the fact that she still had my younger brother living at home and plenty of extended family nearby.

I reached in my purse for a cigarette, then thought better of it. She'd be able to hear me exhale the smoke, and I'd get an earful for sure. "I'm in the middle of a big story and I'm exhausted."

Her voice softened. "So why don't you take a weekend off and fly home?"

"I can't leave right now." I filled her in on the double homicide and funeral.

"You're not driving one of the station's news cars on such a long drive, are you? I hope Jack's there. It's not safe to go alone."

"He's not my cameraman today. But I'm in the Escalade and I'm fine. The station's tracking me on GPS." That last part was a stretch. They had the capability to track me, but I doubted they actually did so most of the time, if at all.

"Thank God."

If she only knew about the real potential danger I was in. I'd intentionally left out any mention of how much I missed home or the ominous notes on my front door. She'd use those details as weapons against my determination to stay in Ashland, and that was a pointless argument. I wasn't leaving.

Mom still didn't understand how important it was for me or any new reporter to work in a small market in order to gain enough experience to get hired on-air in bigger towns. My mother lived under the delusion I could get a reporting gig in Los Angeles without earning it.

"And you got the tires—"

"*Yes,* Mama." It was easier to reassure her that I was safe than argue about why I needed to live far away from home. "I got the tires checked and changed the oil like Dad told me to. I even got my wiper fluid replaced. I'm *fine.*"

Fist-sized dandelions lined the twisting two-lane highway as I rose higher in elevation. I would be hitting a dead zone soon.

Mom exhaled into the phone. "Inna's coming over tonight with her kids. They're growing up so fast."

"Tell her 'hi' for me."

"You know she offered to talk to her anchor friend over at *Good Day LA*."

For as far back as I could remember, my favorite older cousin worked in production for the biggest news station in Los Angeles. She was the one who first made it seem possible I could become a television reporter.

When I didn't respond to Mom's comment, she kept talking. "Inna's happy to talk with Natalie Delisse about getting you a job."

"Mom, it doesn't work that way. It doesn't matter who you know. I still need hands-on experience. Even if I didn't, I don't want everything given to me."

"It doesn't bother you that you may never come home?"

"Of course it does. You think I like being away from my dysfunctional mother?" I really needed a cigarette. Keeping my eyes on the road, I pulled open the handle on the glove compartment and stuck my hand in to fish out a stick of gum, anything to distract me from smoking until I could hang up with my mother. "Are you done with your guilt trip or did you call for an actual reason?"

She let out a long sigh.

"What's wrong?" I asked. "Ouch!" I yanked my finger away from something sharp, blood beading through the valleys on the tip of my skin.

"What's wrong?" Mom's voice raised.

"It's nothing, I stabbed my finger on something in the glove compartment. Don't worry, I'm fine."

"On what?"

Curiosity beat out caution. I kept my eyes on the windy road ahead, and reached my hand in again, carefully touching the smooth edges of a sharp point. It felt like a thorn. Reaching further, I pinched my fingers onto what I guessed was a stem and pulled out a dry, dead red rose.

Silence hummed over the phone in the absence of my answer.

"Are you okay?" Mom persisted.

"Yeah, fine," I lied to keep her quiet.

How did that get in my car? Did I stuff it in there last week when I was drunk? Julien had driven me home, so I never got in my car that night. "What's on your mind, Mom?"

"I had this horrible vision of a tree falling on the road and your car flipping and there was no one around to help you . . ." She droned on with her list of concerns.

I couldn't concentrate.

Where did that rose come from? Did someone break into my car?! Mom kept talking, faster and faster as if she was running from something. She was stalling, I could sense it.

What if the stalker who'd been leaving me notes did this as some sick twisted new message? The thought of it made me so scared, my skin hurt. *Or was I being paranoid?*

"I'm going to lose reception soon." I growled, clearing my clouded thoughts, "Will you spit it out and tell me what's bothering you?"

"Shelby . . . your father has cancer."

The road tunneled through the dense forest. My peripheral vision narrowed to dark, impenetrable tree trunks as my heart caught in my throat.

"It's his prostate," Mom said. "They caught it in the early stages."

"When did you find out?"

"Yesterday."

My mind swirled with panic. Maybe this was all a sign to move home. A sharp wind blasted through the trees, shaking my SUV. The phone line crackled before it went dead.

CHAPTER EIGHT

I followed the highway with eyes that wept like Ashland's autumn rain. From as far back as I could remember, I had craved my dad's attention. I wanted to be the mythical *Daddy's Girl,* the daughter who made her father shine.

Most of the time, I got lost in the shuffle as Dad vied for my spellbinding, often temperamental mother's approval. Despite a costly divorce where my formally middle-income Mom took half, Dad sided with her in nearly every argument, and usually put her needs and wants before mine. But that had changed in the last several years, and now there were so many good memories washed into the mix.

Like the day I decided I was done sneaking out of my bedroom most nights and running with my friends in a tagging crew on the Westside. I'd been getting into turf wars with rival crews, committing lower-level crimes like stealing alcohol from convenient stores and smoking weed at the public park. When I finally told my parents I was going to straighten up and get my GED so I could apply to colleges, Dad immediately began researching the requirements for getting into UCLA. While the rest of the world doubted my ability to make things right, Dad's belief in me helped me believe in myself.

My father and I bonded over late-night binge-watching CNN and Fox News. We debated politics. He was a Republican like Mom, but more centered, and he actually listened and was open to changing his opinions based on my arguments. If we weren't watching the news, Dad and I tuned in to true crime shows and took turns guessing who the killer was behind each sordid tale.

When I landed this job, a profession Dad and I both believed was important and noble, he told everyone his daughter was going to be a television reporter. He loved following my stories and shared the details of my burgeoning career with family and friends.

It was impossible to imagine a life without my dad.

I exited the highway and swerved onto a quiet road. Still no cell service. My heart screamed at me to spin my SUV around and race home to Los Angeles, to my father, to safety.

It would have to wait until morning. Dad would be all right for a few more hours. I'd made a commitment to Melissa's family and I had to be respectful.

Turning right into an overflowing gravel parking lot, I found a space amid the dozens of beater cars and pickup trucks. A sign posted to the sturdy, white rectangular structure read, *Our Lady of Mount Hood Catholic Church*. Fading daylight and an eerie yellow gloom filtered through the overcast sky. The mass had started at 5 p.m. I'd arrived nearly thirty minutes late.

Taking a deep breath to steady myself, I studied my surroundings. Towering pines enveloped the parking lot and beyond. A small country store and an old gas station rested across the street. According to my Google search, the unassuming small church standing before me served this town of approximately seven hundred. Everyone here had to know each other. Everyone had to be feeling the loss of one of their own.

My puffy tear-stained face reflected back at me in the rear-view mirror. Looking away, I ran my hands through my hair and reached over to the passenger side for my purse. I flung the dead rose into the backseat.

Smoothing out my black pants, I forced myself to focus. Melissa Rossi's loved ones were gathered inside, mourning. Judging by the number of vehicles, this church had probably never seen so many people at once. With all the folks who cared about Melissa, it enraged me to think about somebody hurting her so brutally.

I crept inside the ornate Catholic church, awestruck. Rows of wooden pews, overflowing with mourners, lined the sides. A wide colored-concrete walkway ran down the center toward the back wall.

Dozens upon dozens of candles burned. Two glass chandeliers hung from the ceiling. A Virgin Mary, Jesus on the cross, angels, and other religious icons I didn't recognize adorned the walls and stood on elaborate pedestals near the alter. Additional funeral-goers, dressed in black, crowded the back of the standing-room-only space.

I nodded to the corpulent Ashland police officer standing watch near the front door. He turned his head away, ignoring me. Nonetheless, the officer's presence put me slightly more at ease.

I scanned the crowd for Alex Haskell, but couldn't find him. A freckled red-headed man with reading glasses stood on the altar, a microphone grasped in his trembling hand. His voice shook, his pale face wet with tears as he struggled to get through his speech.

Judging by his resemblance, I gathered the man was Melissa Rossi's dad. "Melissa was our tough cookie, my fighter, my survivor. We never needed to be worried about her," he choked through tears.

Not wanting to break any rules, I'd left my bulky camera equipment in the car and made the decision not to record any of the service on my cell phone. Instead, I pulled out my reporter's notebook and stood quiet, listening.

"When Melissa was sixteen, she survived a near-fatal car accident. She broke both her legs, an arm, her back, and the truck crushed her skull, she was never supposed to have walked or talked again."

The microphone let out a high-pitched screech and Mr. Rossi's head jerked back in shock. It toned back down, allowing him to continue. "My daughter wasn't having any of that. We couldn't get her away from school, she begged us to homeschool her during an intense year of physical therapy. She didn't want to fall behind because she was determined to graduate with Liberty so they could go to OSU together. Melissa made as full of a recovery as she could've. It was an honest-to-God miracle." Mr. Rossi's face crumpled. Men, women, and children sobbed.

Outrage burned in my eyes, bringing me back to tears. Melissa had fought for her life with a fierce determination, only to be knifed to death. I wanted to tear apart the monster who killed her.

Mr. Rossi rocked back and forth on the altar. "Melissa didn't let anything stop her. She wasn't able to run track anymore, but we couldn't keep her away from the stands to cheer on her friends. She graduated with honors, tutored other students. She busted her butt and got into Southern Oregon University on a full-ride scholarship. She wanted to use her second chance to the fullest. Melissa earned a degree in biology and got her dream job as a health inspector. She wanted to make sure people could be safe anywhere they went. Just a few months ago, we threw a big party at our home, full of family and friends who loved her, to celebrate the seventh anniversary, her lucky number, of what we called her 'Live Day'. I'll always remember the look on her face that day, so full of gratitude and hope for her future."

Thoughts of my dad pushed back into my head. What if this funeral were for him? Or if my paranoia rang true, for me? For the first time, I allowed the icy reality to cut through me. If my stalker was the killer, I could be next.

A cool sweat trickled down the inside of my blouse. My stomach lurched as I dashed out of the church door to be sick in the bushes.

———

"Are you okay?"

I turned to see Liberty's face crinkled in concern. She stood holding her fiancé, Brandon's, hand.

"Yeah, sorry."

"Here's a tissue," she offered. "I always have one handy these days."

"Thanks." I wiped my mouth and gave Brandon a nod. He pushed back his long blond bangs and stared at the ground.

The outline of the moon shined in the darkening sky, and a brisk evening breeze blew through my hair. Liberty tucked a loose strand of her own straggly brown curls behind her ear before looking at me with her wide gray eyes. "You know for the viewing they dressed her in a turtleneck? She hated turtlenecks. She refused to wear one when she was alive."

I touched my own throat, imagining the reason for a high collar.

Liberty squeezed Brandon's arm, as if holding on to him anchored her. "Melissa was the toughest girl I ever knew."

"I bet," I said, crumbling the tissue in my hand.

"Anyway, we're getting ready to head over to the Rossis' house along with a bunch of Melissa's family and friends. My poor fiancé's almost a bigger wreck than I am right now. He's been having nightmares all week. And I'm sure you noticed Melissa's mom couldn't even be here. It was too much. But she wants you to see where Melissa grew up. You should drive over."

The hushed sounds of voices comforting one another floated from the front steps of the church. Gravel crunched under mourners' feet as they walked toward their cars.

The shaking in my hands calmed. "Sure. I've got the address. I'll catch up with you soon. Is Alex Haskall here?"

Liberty shook her head. "Melissa's mom told me to ask him to stay home. He and Melissa were broken up anyway."

Even if I disagreed, I couldn't blame the family. Alex's DNA results weren't back yet. Everyone was a suspect, and boyfriends and ex-boyfriends always topped the list until proven innocent.

I nodded, not knowing what to say.

"Mr. Rossi needs to talk to you." She pointed to where he stood. "He wants to make a plea to anyone who watches your story."

"Oh," I said in surprise.

"Yeah. I'll see you later." She and Brandon stepped away as Mr. Rossi approached.

"Mr. Rossi?" I extended my hand. "I'm so sorry for your loss. I can't even imagine how hard today is for you. And for Mrs. Rossi . . ." my voice trailed off. How would my mother hold up if it had been me?

Mr. Rossi's pale face stiffened with resolve. "What matters now is we find who did this."

"Of course. Liberty said you wanted to make a plea to the public. Did you want to talk on camera or would you prefer I write something into my story?"

"On camera."

"Okay." I attached a small mic to my cell phone and pressed the record button. Without asking him to say or spell his name or state who he was, I began talking. "Mr. Arnold Rossi, is there anything you want to tell our viewers about your daughter?"

"Melissa was a good girl. We need to find the person who did this. It's the only thing that matters anymore."

"Is there anyone you can think of who could've wanted to harm her?"

"Not at all. Melissa was a sweet girl, she went to work, spent time with her friends; she had a quiet life." His hands tightened into fists. "The police need to look closer at the men in her roommate's circle. Daphne had a different sort of lifestyle, the kind that invited any kind of person into my daughter's home. Have you had the chance to talk to

Daphne's mom or anyone from her family? We haven't received a single word from them. Mrs. Rossi would like to hear from Daphne's mom."

"I spoke with one of Daphne's friends online. Daphne's mom is flying in after her daughter's funeral next week to speak with the police in person. She's a single mom going through this from across the country. I'm sure she's doing her best just to make it through each day."

"Did she say if she had any idea who might've done this?"

"Everybody thinks it must be someone Daphne knew, but her friends say Daphne only dated nice guys. She wanted to settle down, she was obsessing over getting married."

Mr. Rossi's shoulders slumped. "Melissa wanted to get married too."

"I'm so sorry." I stared at the gravel beneath my feet, feeling uncomfortable and unsure what else to say. "Is there anything you'd like to add to our interview?"

"No." He shoved his hands in his trouser pockets. "I wasn't there to protect my baby girl. I failed her. But you know what's worse than having your child killed?"

"No sir, what is that?"

"It's not knowing who did it, or why."

"Everyone involved in this case cares about your daughter and Daphne. I've never seen anything like it." I searched for the best words to help. "Someone is going to figure this out soon. I promise."

Mr. Rossi's red hair lay defeated, flat against his skull. His face looked gaunt and dark circles underscored his tired eyes. "Please help us find out who is responsible."

I looked away again, distracting myself by fiddling with

the camera on my cell phone. Melissa and Daphne felt like friends. We were the same age, living in the same town, on our own and away from our families. We were all pursuing careers that meant something special to us. We might even have the same killer coming after us.

I'd never cared more about a story I was covering than I did right now. If I could, I would've reached out and hugged Melissa's dad. But that wouldn't be professional, and it would also likely cause me to break down completely.

Instead, I mumbled a thank-you for the interview before one of Mr. Rossi's sons moved in to wrap an arm around his dad. I moved away to give them their privacy and shoot some video of the crowd dispersing, along with some footage of the church. When I finished, I zipped up my jacket for extra warmth and climbed into the protection of my SUV. Before I typed up the story or filed a quick live report on Instagram, I set aside my pride and texted Jack.

It didn't matter what he'd done with Kaya or that he was mad at me. I was tired of putting up emotional barriers and pushing away my true feelings. I needed Jack.

I sent him a text:

Me: Hey.

He replied within seconds.

Jack: What's up? How was the funeral?

Me: It wasn't great, Jack.

Jack: Want to go out and talk about it?

Me: I'm still wrapping up the story. Need to get some extra shots and a few more interviews before heading back to the station. The show's over at 11. Is that good?

Jack: Sure, Shelbs. Meet me at Leela Thai at midnight?

Me: Perfect.

Knowing I would see him soon would get me through the next several hours.

CHAPTER NINE

The November night lay silent, save for the trickle of the meandering creek and a subtle wind that blew through the trees. As planned, Jack and I met up at the Thai restaurant and decided to walk across the street to Lithia Park; Ashland, Oregon's version of Central Park. Surrounded by nearly one hundred acres of forested canyonland, this place felt almost magical.

As on edge as I was to be out at night with a potential stalker watching us, I felt safe with Jack. I was probably being stupid, but if I couldn't have the Pacific Ocean to cleanse my tortured soul, Jack, and Lithia Park, with its graceful Japanese maples, sculpted rose garden, and enchanting trails, was a pleasurable second best.

"Thanks for waiting up late." I passed Jack a cigarette and lit one for myself. As I inhaled that first drag and felt the smoke go down my lungs, a warm buzzing feeling ran through my veins, soothing my body.

"Late? It's a Saturday." He lounged on the swing next to mine.

Blue-white smoke curled and folded off the tip of my

cigarette and into the night air. "Thank you for waiting, anyway." I hated how awkward our conversation felt.

Leaning back, I swung my legs for momentum, desperate to put all of the day's misery on pause and unwind in Jack's presence.

"Are you cold?" he asked. "You want my jacket?"

"I'm good." Since moving to the Pacific Northwest, I'd built up a tolerance for cold weather. My jeans and the fluffy white pullover I'd changed into provided the perfect amount of warmth and comfort.

"How'd the funeral go?"

"I mean, it was a funeral." My swing took flight and I sailed through the darkness. "I interviewed Melissa Rossi's dad and some of her friends. CNN picked up the feed. They want to use my story."

"Really? So you're going to be on CNN?"

"Well, no. They didn't want to talk to me, but they're going to use my interviews and video. So that's pretty cool."

"That's great." He wound himself around in a circle, twisting the swing's metal chains into tight coils.

"Jack?"

"Yeah?"

"I'm sorry about the other night. I was kind of acting like a jerk."

"I'm over it." Jack allowed the swing to unwind itself. "Can I ask you a question though, about something you said?"

"Sure." Any conversation that didn't include unbearable small talk, or relate to my family or fears, was a welcomed distraction. "But first I want some of those edibles I know you have on you."

He grinned. "No secrets in a newsroom, I guess."

I could feel my eyes twinkle with mischief. "Newsroom? I'm an investigative reporter—you can't hide from me. Plus, I'm your best friend, so there's no escaping."

"Well, Jinkies, I guess I can't get past you, Velma." In response, he reached into his front jean pocket and pulled out a small plastic baggie stuffed with gummy bears. "What's your favorite color?" he asked.

"Orange, red, and green. I'll take three."

"Three?! Why don't you start with a leg?"

I dragged my feet in the sand to slow my roll. "Since I already ate one of my own before I came here, I'll settle for two." I put out my hand.

"How about only one more then, we'll see how you take it."

"Fine."

"One of us needs to be somewhat coherent. I'll start with half." He chuckled, handing me a bright red gummy bear.

Jack made it hard not to smile. I popped the gummy in my mouth. "So?" I asked.

"Yeah?"

"What's the question you were going to ask me?"

He rubbed the back of his neck. "What's your deal with bad boys?"

"Ah." I giggled, my hair flying behind me. I pumped my legs again, rising and falling, swinging higher and higher. "It's less complicated when you're dating guys who don't give a shit about you."

"What do you mean? You want to date people who don't care about you?"

"No, it's not that. It's, you know, they don't care about anything. They don't get mad if you have to bail for work. They don't stress if you don't text back right away. No expectations, no getting hurt—just a hookup."

"That doesn't sound very upstanding of you, Ms. Day."

"It's not." I took a quick puff on my cigarette, relieved the rush of air hadn't blown it out. "Enough about me. What's your story, Jack Miller? Why'd you get so upset when Lily brought up San Diego?"

"I just don't like to talk about it."

"Fair enough. Why'd you choose Ashland? You never told me."

"The space between things is bigger here." He drew a puff of his cigarette, blowing smoke out his nose.

I thought about my home in LA, how everybody everywhere was so smashed together. Oregon was nice, spacious. You had room to breathe in the world around you. It just wasn't my speed.

"Would you ever go back? Not just to San Diego, but somewhere in SoCal?"

"Why, you heading that way?"

"I've been thinking about it. More than usual." I wrapped my lips around my cigarette for another pull.

"It'd be hard to leave Ashland." He blew out a thick trail of blue-white smoke. "Good fishing, lots of mountain bike trails."

I started to feel dizzy. It was difficult to tell if it was the swinging or the first round of my edibles kicking in. "You're such a mountain man."

"I'm all about it. But sure, I'd go back home. For the right reason."

"Sometimes I want to pack up and take off." I tried to sound lighthearted. "How about we go? Tonight?"

Pressing his lips into a fine line of doubt, he asked, "What's up, Shelbs? Something's on your mind."

A lump formed in my throat, making it hurt to swallow. I wanted to tell him about my dad's cancer, about the frightening notes and the dead rose, about how confused I felt about staying here. But I was still scared to make myself fully vulnerable. I wasn't good at relationships. My therapist called it "self-sabotaging tendencies".

So I changed the subject. "Melissa Rossi's family likes me. So does the lead police sergeant. Maybe someone I talk to will know something that will help solve the case. I could do something good in this world. Something that matters."

Jack took a drag on his cigarette and blew the smoke away from me. "You care."

"I feel a connection to those women, especially Daphne. Everyone's pointing fingers and treating her like a whore because she dated around. From what I can tell, she only wanted to settle down."

"Sometimes you can't win," he said.

"No kidding. She left her mother and moved all the way across the country because she knew what she wanted, bigger opportunities, better options. She came here with guts. She took the shot. She was feminist as hell." I flung myself back farther and kicked out my legs, flying higher than I thought the swing could take me. "All the judgement over her choices. I can totally relate to her."

"I think you're both lost." Jack took one last drag on his cigarette before stubbing it out on the bottom of his shoe. "Well, she *was* lost. You still are."

My upper lip snarled at the ridiculousness of his comment. "Lost? What, you think I'm a Lost Girl? I bet Daphne Deluca knew exactly what she wanted, and I know what I want too. From what her friends say, she was determined to settle down and get married. I'm chasing a top-market career in journalism without any of my parents' money or help. Different goals, but the same focus and drive."

"Like a hamster on a wheel."

My mouth fell open. "Seriously?"

"You're so bent on making it to the bigs, you don't care about what really matters. Look how short life was for Daphne. She probably did everything right to find the perfect guy and have the perfect life, and for what?" Jack stuck his cigarette butt in his back pocket. "You're so busy chasing things you think are going to make you happy, you're missing it all. Everything you need is right in front of you. It's already here."

The cold blew through my sweater and penetrated my bones. Jack had no idea what I was going through or what my priorities were. "Right in front of me? Like what? Like you? Is that what you're getting at? 'Cause—"

"Did you stop by Crater Lake on your way to the funeral?"

"Did I? What? No, I was working."

"Have you visited there at all?" Jack's long dark hair shimmered in the moonlight when he pulled it behind his head only to let it fall loose through his fingers and brush back onto his shoulders.

"I haven't had time."

"It's one of the seven natural wonders of Oregon." He lifted his eyebrows at me. "Did you know it's the deepest, bluest lake in the United States? It's one of the most amazing places in the world and you've never even bothered to check it out."

I didn't respond.

"This is the stuff I'm taking about, Shelby. It's like your whole identity is wrapped up in your career and you're so busy working, you're missing out on life."

"Fine then, let's check out the creek." I launched off my swing and bent my knees upon landing. It was time to change up the scenery.

Jack flew off his swing and landed next to me.

"Oh, my God." I laughed. "What are you, Spiderman?"

When we reached the water, something came over me. My stifled heart needed to feel something. I didn't care that it was a near freezing Oregon night, I needed to feel alive.

Kicking off my shoes, I slid out of my white sports socks and shoved one inside each shoe.

"What are you doing?" Jack's brow crinkled with amusement.

"Seeing how far I can make it up the creek. Take off your shoes, you wouldn't want to miss out on beating me across, would you?"

Jack gave an exasperated laugh. "I need to get high with you more often. You really lighten up." He unlaced his black Vans.

"We'll have a better grip if we're barefoot," I said.

"And our shoes won't get wet when we fall. You know it's dark outside, right? And the water is ice. And you're pretty high."

"There's plenty of moonlight. What's wrong?" I teased. "I thought you were a surfer. You telling me you're afraid of a little cold water?"

"I'm *afraid* you're going to wipe out." He smirked, taking my sneakers and holding them in his hands. "I better hold on to these. You never know when a feral hippie's gonna show up and steal your stuff."

I grinned at him, ignoring the sarcasm in his voice. "Everybody thinks it's all peace and love with those people, but I get a bad vibe from them. You watch, if they don't catch the murderer soon, this whole town's gonna turn on those creeps."

Ignoring my comment, Jack motioned toward the creek. "Lead the way."

I gently tapped my left foot against a smooth rock near the edge of the waterbed. Ice-cold creek water rushed around it on all sides, numbing my skin. It was exactly what I needed.

I placed my full weight on my left foot as my right foot reached out to the next closest dry rock. "Coming?" I waved Jack onward.

"Right behind you."

I turned and watched him step from rock to rock. "You're good at this."

"You might have noticed..." he tucked a wayward strand of his hair behind his ear, "I'd follow you anywhere."

"What the—" I stood on a fat rock and in a marijuana-induced, slow-motion haze, I tried to move the muscles in my face.

"What's up?" He leaped forward until he landed on my rock and fixed his eyes on mine.

I puckered my lips out like a duck.

"What?" he asked again, looking completely confused.

"I can totally lift my upper lip on the right side of my face, but not on my left side."

I could feel his warmth beside me.

"Show me," he said.

I laughed at his seriousness. Even I knew I wasn't making much sense. He watched as I made a dramatic smiley face.

"There," he said, "you just smiled evenly so I guess you can lift both sides."

"Yeah, but not the same amount. It's lopsided."

"Is this a new problem?"

"No." I shook my head. "I think I've always been this way."

"Then, it's not like you had a stroke or something."

I giggled again. "I guess not."

"Girl, you are stoned to the bone."

"Only a little bit. Oh, man, these edibles are intense." A thought occurred to me. "Wait, you're not trying to use truth serum on me, are you?"

He tilted his head in thought. "What are you hiding?"

"Whatever." I leaped away from him to the next rock and nearly fell in the rushing water.

"What's up that you haven't told me?" Jack persisted.

"It's not a big deal."

"Like what?" he asked.

"Nothing major."

"So then tell me."

My head floated above my neck, loose and free like a helium balloon. No inhibitions, I was tired of holding everything inside. I decided I wanted to talk. "What do you want to know?"

"You asked me to pack up and leave with you, Shelbs. What's really bothering you?"

I spit it out before I had time to stop myself. "My mom called to tell me my dad is sick. They just found out."

The muscles in Jack's jaw tensed. "What's wrong with him?"

"Prostate cancer. Stage one."

He tugged at his earlobe in thought. "They caught it early."

We stood only a few feet apart, looking into one another, each of us on our own rock, surrounded by gurgling creek water. "I talked to my dad tonight on my drive back from the funeral. I was ready to quit my job and run home to take care of him. But I guess there's nothing for me to do. My mom already scheduled surgery for next week. As far as the doctors can tell, the cancer hasn't spread. Chances are they'll get rid of it completely."

"Will he need radiation or chemotherapy?"

"Probably not." I dipped my big toe into the frigid water and held it there until it hurt. "I told you my parents have been divorced for almost seventeen years, but of course Mom's moving him into the spare bedroom in our house. She already hired my old nanny to look after him. Dad says he'll be fine, everything's handled."

Jack's eyebrows squished together. "You almost look disappointed."

"I wanted to be there for him. I'm his daughter."

"Of course you do."

"My mom always does this, she steps in and takes over completely. She doesn't leave any breathing room for the rest of us. And you know what?" I was really letting down my guard now, airing my wounds. "It's total crap. Growing up, most of the time she treated him worse than the hired help. But it never mattered. Whoever else she dated, whatever cruel words she flung both to Dad's face and behind his back, his love never wavered.

"He bought her jewelry on special occasions, worked out with her at his private gym several days a week, and even lunched with her at the country club on weekends, all on his dime, like they were still married. For nine years, he rented an apartment around the corner from our house, just hoping she would invite him to move back in with us.

"Up until recently, nothing I did distracted him from her. I always came in second, my younger brother a faded third. And now he's sick, and of course, my mom is everything he needs."

"Why don't you take some time and go down there and visit him?"

I shook my head. "My dad said if I don't stay here and investigate such a big story, I could miss something. If he doesn't want me there, it's better I stay in Ashland and prove myself. Sometimes, I think this job means more to him than it does to me."

"Why would reporting be more important to him than it is to you?"

"It's nothing. I don't really care."

Before Jack could respond, I leapt, landing from rock, to rock, to rock. "Come on, slow poke," I called. "Keep up."

Jack bolted forward, taking on the oversized stones to catch me. "You move around like you've done this before."

"I guess that means you can't give me a hard time again about missing out on the recreational joys of the great outdoors, can you?" I giggled, laughing off the heaviness of my previous rant. "Maybe, I don't spend all of my free time working after all."

"Sure, whatever. Let's head up by that next bridge, there's a place I want to show you." Jack jumped past me and then moved forward a few rocks. "I thought you could keep up, Shelbs."

Five rocks later he pointed up the slope from the creek bed to the right.

"Oh, wow." I couldn't help but stare. "It's beautiful."

A gazebo stood beside the arched bridge crossing over Lithia Creek, lit with small round white bulbs. A mild breeze blew through the trees, ruffling the branches, propelling tiny yellow leaves to flutter gracefully in the lit space.

For a moment, I felt a cold shiver of fear, like someone was watching us in the woods. Jack reached out for my hand and I pushed away my worry. Forget fear, at least for tonight.

"Why do you want my hand?" I asked, remaining planted on my rock, a small smile spreading to my cheeks.

"I need to do something."

"What?" I asked.

"Dance with you, of course."

"Did you plan this?" My smile spread wider.

"It was *your* idea to jump around in the creek at night in November. We got lucky, it's usually not lit up like this."

He led me out of the water and up the side of the gentle slope. The cool wet grass leading to the gazebo tickled my bare feet.

"You're not too high, right?" he asked, leading me up the steps to the wooden platform. "You're stumbling."

My defenses were down, I was finally ready for whatever happened next. "I'm fine."

Jack set down our shoes and pulled out his phone. Ed Sheeran's *Perfect* spilled forth. I opened my mouth to speak, but Jack rested his strong hands on the curve of my back, and I forgot what I was going to say.

Lithia Creek trickled over its waterbed. Tree branches rustled against one another, back and forth as we swayed in time with the music. Small steps to the rhythm.

I rested my head on Jack's broad chest, he smelled like citrus and fresh pine. I loved how much bigger he was than me, how he cared so deeply.

"Why do you put up with me?" I asked.

Jack's full lips parted. "Because everywhere I go, I wish you were there."

"That's pretty sweet," I said, my heart flushing with unexpected joy, preparing to cross carefully guarded lines.

He held steady eye contact, skimming his thumb along my cheek. "You're beautiful."

I smiled back at him.

He listened. He cared. He put others first. Jack was worth the risk of letting go. Any woman would be lucky to have him.

He spoke softly, "And you have the cutest little freckle on the edge of your upper lip."

Jack pressed closer. I could feel my body tense with anticipation as his warm hand gently tilted my chin up. Any remaining resistance dissolved. I leaned forward slowly and kissed him. His lips against mine, so intoxicating I forgot to breathe.

CHAPTER TEN

I strolled into the near empty newsroom Sunday morning still riding the high of last night's kiss. I'd let down my defenses with Jack and was already falling hard. When he walked me home sometime around 3 a.m., we made plans to meet up later this afternoon. I could hardly wait to see him.

Smoothing out my soft gray leggings, I nodded a hello to Kaya who sat clueless at the assignment desk playing with a rubber band. It was time to focus, I was here again on my day off to do something important.

Daphne's close friend had tuned in to CNN last night and caught my coverage of Melissa's funeral, specifically my interview with Melissa Rossi's dad who had said Daphne's lifestyle probably attributed to the murders. The friend encouraged Daphne's mom to reach out to me on Facebook earlier this morning and we'd scheduled a video-chat interview for as soon as I got into the station. Daphne's mom wanted to squelch the rumors that any of this was somehow her daughter's fault.

I opened my computer in the private conference room and logged onto Skype to record our interview. Waiting dutifully for 11 o'clock on the dot, once the time changed, I hit the call button and listened to the happy buzz of the dial tone.

Evangeline Pitzer's pretty heart-shaped face popped on to the video screen. "Miss Day, can you see me?"

"Yes, I can see you perfectly." I nodded encouragingly at Daphne's mom. Even with her dark hair tied back in a loose ponytail and worry lines written all over her grieving face, her big green eyes and high cheekbones struck a stunning resemblance to Daphne. It broke my heart to think that every time Evangeline looked in the mirror, she would see her deceased daughter.

"Thank you so much for talking with me. It's very brave of you to do this," I said, taking a deep inhale as the warm memories of my night with Jack faded. The protective pieces of me that had fought so hard to stifle an emotional connection to any of my stories had lost this battle. I'd given up trying. Just like with Jack, my heart was invested.

"Thank you, Miss Day." Evangeline dotted the corner of her eyes with a tissue. "I wanted to tell you about my Daphne. She was a bright light to everyone who knew her. It's not right what people are saying about her. She doesn't deserve any of this."

"Not at all." I bit at the inside of my cheek. It'd barely been two weeks since her daughter's murder, and Evangeline now had to endure the rumors about Daphne's lifestyle. "Evangeline, I want you to know, it's just you and me talking. There's no one else in this room, and if there's anything you don't want me to use, let me know and I'll edit it out."

"Thank you." She touched the tiny gold cross on her neck.

"You can also stop this at any time," I assured her, adjusting the volume on our video chat. "If you're ready, can you tell us a little bit about your daughter?"

"Sure. Are you recording?"

"I am."

Her lips trembled as she found her words. "Daphne was our shining little star. She loved singing and cooking and spending time with her friends and family. We all adored her, and we didn't have much but, we gave her everything we could, my mom and dad and me. Her brother, too. She was so kind and wonderful and just the center of our world."

"She sounds like a lucky girl," I said, instantly regretting using the word lucky to describe a woman who'd been stabbed to death.

Evangeline blinked tears from her eyes, then began talking again. "When Daphne was a little girl, all she wanted to do was take care of her younger brother and baby cousins. She would tell anybody who would listen that when she grew up, she wanted to be a TV reporter."

"She wanted to be a journalist?" I slipped off my black button-down sweater, feeling a rush of heat. The more I learned about her, the more Daphne reminded me of myself, it was yet another piece of this girl I would never meet.

"She did." Evangeline smiled at the memory. "Wherever she went she used to carry a little microphone in one hand and a baby doll in the other. Daphne would interview my parents and anyone else she could corral into giving her the time of day. All day, every day, she'd get her microphone and sing, 'Ladies and Gentlemen, Daphne presents the Daphne News.' We couldn't get enough of it. She wanted to do everything. For a while in high school Daphne was intent on becoming a teacher, but she got a job doing PR at the Shakespeare Festival. She always loved being around the arts."

This was my opportunity to segue to the men in Daphne's life. I had to go there, too many people were thinking about it for me to ignore Daphne's show-stopping good looks and active love life. It was better that her mother address it head-on. "Everybody probably loved her, she was a beautiful girl, she probably got a lot of attention."

Evangeline pressed her hand to her heart. "Wherever Daphne went she turned heads. And it's true, men loved her, she was a natural heartbreaker. She never wanted to hurt anybody, but there were a lot of men who fell in love with her and wanted her to be their one and only."

"Do you know of anyone who wasn't able to win her over and would want to hurt her?"

"She would break up with boys, but most of the time they would stay friends. I'm sure there were some who wished they could have stayed with her instead of breaking up, but they didn't hold a grudge."

"Is it possible any of them felt like if they couldn't have her, no one could?"

Evangeline shook her head. "She didn't complain about it, not to me, anyway. I thought she told me everything, but some of her girlfriends have come forward with stories."

I leaned in a little closer. "Like what?"

"Well, there was a boy she dated for several months when she first moved out there, but I guess his dad was acting inappropriately. He called her on the phone one day and invited her on a vacation to Cabo with only him. Daphne broke it off with that guy. She didn't want to be with someone whose dad was making passes at her. The boy took it hard and had been sending her gifts in the mail and messaging her online. She had to block him on everything and change her phone number. He wouldn't let it go. Daphne's girlfriends are a little suspicious of both that boy as well as his dad."

"Do the police know about this?"

"Yes, Daphne's girlfriends told them about him. There was another gentleman too. He bought Daphne a new car as a surprise. It was too much, she wouldn't take it. He tried to give her more things and it was starting to make her uncomfortable. She didn't want to take advantage of a man like that."

Maybe, it really was best to focus the investigation on the men in Daphne's life. "Wow," I said, "she really did attract a lot of attention."

Evangeline ducked her head to blow her nose off-camera. "Daphne saw the best in everyone. She was so positive. You know, in the past week, so many of her friends have called with their condolences. They all thought of her as a best friend. She was one of those people who, when you talked to her, she made you feel like you were her whole world. She made people feel special." She bit her lip, even though it still trembled, and blinked back tears.

I shifted in my chair before asking another difficult question. "That special presence she had must have helped her win beauty pageants." It was a salacious detail people loved to point out, as if winning a beauty contest made her a vapid predator.

Her mom's eyebrows pinched together in sorrow. "Daphne only tried out for two pageants for scholarship money. As beautiful as she was, she wasn't built like a typical model; she was short and curvy. Daphne didn't take home Ms. Alabama, but she was named Ms. Gadsden."

I dug deeper. "I have to ask, what do you say to anyone who thinks that Daphne was dating too many men, or she was using her good looks to land a rich husband?"

Her mom's eyes went wide before she recovered. Smoothing strands of hair back toward her ponytail, she stared into the camera. "You know, it's easy to look at someone as attractive and sweet-tempered as Daphne and think, this girl has it too easy, she doesn't suffer like the rest of us.

"Her beauty was a gift from God, and people have been jealous of her for this her whole life. But the truth is, you don't know someone's struggle just by looking at them. Sure, she kept a smile on her pretty face. What they don't see is her history." Evangeline blew at her nose again.

"As Daphne blossomed, I would tell her, 'it's just as easy to marry a rich man as it is a poor man. Least if they take off on you the way your father did, you'll have two pennies to rub together.' But she wouldn't hear it. That girl gives everyone she likes an equal chance. She only wants to replace what she didn't have, a stable home. She's looking for true love, plain and simple."

I couldn't help noticing Evangeline had slipped into the present tense. Her daughter's death probably wasn't real to her yet. "I can only imagine how devastating this is for everyone."

Evangeline pushed her fingers over her temples. "I guess I feel numb most of the time. You don't want to believe it's true. The pain, when it does come, it hurts so bad. It's too much to bear." Tears fell down her face.

"I'm so sorry." I could feel my nose sting and my eyes burn with regret for her profound loss.

I made another silent pledge to write the most compelling story I could put together. Evangeline's powerful soundbites about her loss would connect with viewers. Perhaps CNN would pick the entire story and make it national. If it went viral, we could get the support of a nation, and we'd be one step closer to putting these girls to rest.

CHAPTER ELEVEN

Doing my best to leave work emotions behind, I stood in front of *Leela Thai* on Main Street, inhaling the deeply satisfying scents of ginger and basil. I straightened the small sapphire ring my grandmother had given me, fidgeting with anticipation in the brisk November air. Jack had suggested we meet here to go mountain biking on one of the Alice in Wonderland Trails above Lithia Park.

Squinting into the afternoon sun, searching for Jack's handsome face, the occasional passerby smiled and nodded hello. Tourist season was coming to an end. Only small handfuls of diehard Shakespeare lovers remained; wandering downtown, shopping at our upmarket boutiques, and grabbing designer lunches at restaurants that easily rivaled those in any major metropolitan city.

Come on Jack, I glanced around, *where are you?* Delicate butterflies flapped inside my stomach. I'd packaged my story for the evening show and made the decision to turn off my cell and fully enjoy the rest of my day off.

"You made it," Jack's deep voice called out.

I turned to see him smiling at me like he'd found his way home.

My heart beat faster at the sight of him. He looked even more appealing than usual in black basketball shorts and a long cornflower blue thermal T-shirt that matched the color of his eyes. I wanted to touch his stubbled face, raise my lips to his, and kiss him like we did last night. My barriers had tumbled, I was falling for him.

Instead, I took a deep breath and gave him a shy smile. "I told you I'd come."

"I thought the city girl might find a way to back out of a day in the dirt."

I looked at the two bikes he guided, one handlebar gripped in each of his sturdy hands. Helmets hung from the free handles. "Wasn't it my idea to jump around in the creek last night?" I nervously twirled a loose lock of golden-brown hair around my index finger. "And, if I remember correctly, weren't you the one who'd hesitated?"

"Hey, now." He chuckled in a low rumble. "I was only concerned about you falling in."

"It's actually pretty chilly out today. Feels like it dropped a few degrees in temperature." I hugged myself as a small wind picked up, dragging the final gasps of autumn's orange and gold leaves in its wake.

"If you want me to walk these back home," he motioned to the bikes, "we can totally do something else. I'm happy to be hanging out with you. It doesn't matter what we do."

"No." I put my hand on the smaller of the two bicycles, the red one that belonged to his roommate's girlfriend. "Let's go for it."

"Cool." He pushed the bike closer toward me and let go.

I gripped the handle tighter than necessary and peered into the street, edging away from the sidewalk as I searched both ways for traffic. "Ready?"

Jack took a hesitant step to follow me before stopping. "I got you something."

I looked back at him, smiling in surprise. "Really? Why?"

"Because it made me think of you." He pulled a small canvas satchel out of his pocket, marked with delicate black lettering: *Peace Love Planet.* "I saw it at the artisans market this morning, nothing fancy."

I watched in anticipation as he loosened the drawstrings and pulled out a pink beaded bracelet with a small pinkish-beige sea turtle etched into a single stone.

"I remember you said you loved seeing the turtles swimming whenever you went to Hawaii with your family. And the proceeds are supposed to go toward cleaning the ocean," he said, letting the bracelet dangle before me in his fingers.

I could feel my face flush with unexpected heat. "It's so pretty. I can't believe you bought me a gift."

"Here, let me put it on you."

"Yes, please." I reached out my hand and he slipped the bracelet over my fingers and onto my tiny wrist. His fresh scent and his warmth so close, I watched Jack carefully adjust the beads. We stood there, our hands touching, neither one of us letting go.

"Thank you," I broke the trance. "It's beautiful." Slivers of fear mixed with exhilaration. I owned a lot of expensive jewelry thanks to my mom and dad, but this gift felt truly special, maybe too special.

"Anything would look beautiful on you," he said, his

blue eyes gazing into mine until I looked away and prepared to cross Main Street.

———

We pedaled to the base of a steep dirt pathway surrounded by tall majestic pines densely populating both sides of the trail. "It smells like Christmas," I said to Jack as we stopped and assessed the path.

He placed his right foot on his pedal, ready to launch. "My favorite holiday."

"I'm more of a Hanukkah kind of girl." I tightened the straps on my small backpack, feeling proud of myself for packing us water bottles and some trail mix.

He adjusted his helmet and looked over at me. "Tell me the story again of how you changed your last name. Wasn't your mom against it?"

I lifted my right foot off the ground and pressed the pedal, thinking I'd better get moving again before I changed my mind. The incline ahead taunted my nerves. Mountain biking was completely out of my comfort zone. "No, it was my dad. He couldn't understand why I wanted something generic for work. Like Rosenberg didn't immediately identify me as different. My dad's never lived outside of Los Angeles, he doesn't get it."

I started pedaling, my thigh muscles immediately burning in protest.

Jack began riding. "Sometimes I wish I could blend in a little easier." It felt like two seconds passed before he shot several feet ahead of me. "Did I tell you that last week while I was standing in line at a gas station in Redding, a guy walked in and yelled out to me, 'put $20 on five'? Like he assumed because I'm brown, I worked there. When I looked at him in confusion, he said 'gracias' and walked back out to his car."

"He seriously assumed by looking at you that you speak Spanish and must be the gas attendant? What a joke. You should have told him *Mazel Tov*, just to mess with him." I huffed, already out of breath, "That's exactly why I didn't want to go by Shelby Rosenberg. People make assumptions. Also, who wants to be the token Jew covering every single Festival of Lights story and speaking on behalf of 'my people' like a United Nations' ambassador?"

"At least they'd get your heritage correct."

I pedaled harder, giving it my all, even if I thought it might kill me. *Pain is weakness leaving the body.* "That guy who said that to you was a moron."

Jack let off the pedals so I could catch up. "It's not that big a deal. I'm used to it."

I could hear Lithia Creek flowing down below us. Moss grew over the bases of the trunks like a fairy tale world, and smooth rocks lined our path. I had to admit, Jack was right about the things I'd been missing out on while I chased down leads. Ashland was even more magnificent than I'd realized.

Jack breathed easily, like pedaling straight up a vertical hill was effortless. "My mom used to say how much she loved that her married name was so common: Josephine Miller. Maybe she wanted to blend in too. Guess there's benefits to marrying a white guy."

Jack's mom had developed diabetes a few years back and she didn't trust doctors or modern medicine. She saw a spiritual healer in Los Angeles, perhaps staying true to her Native American roots. Unfortunately, her condition got worse and her liver stopped functioning. She died a few months before Jack left San Diego.

"Sucks that you can't call her up and ask her," I said, feeling an enormous wave of sadness. Whenever I thought of Jack's loss, it made me feel guilty for sweating the small stuff.

"I miss her all time," he slowed down even more, allowing me to pedal closer, "but I still talk to her. She just doesn't always answer."

A bird cried out from the trees.

"I'm so sorry, Jack."

"Don't be. It's not your fault."

My bike lined up with his, and we pedaled in tandem as I gave it my all to appear at ease.

"You never said so, but I figured your mom's the reason you moved here. You know, to get a fresh start. I didn't want to say anything in front of Lily and them. It's none of their business."

Jack's eyes focused on the trail ahead. "No. It was more than that." He crept ahead of me without trying.

I gulped for air, my pace falling behind. Cigarettes were destroying my lungs. "I bet she's watching over us right now."

"Yeah." He slowed down with me. "She was a beautiful woman. I wish you could've met her."

"Me too." Anyone who had raised such a kind son had to be a decent person. Stopping my bike, I fetched the water bottle from my backpack. Jack put his feet on the ground to wait for me. "I can't imagine losing a parent." I offered him water, eager to change the subject before I got too emotional.

He searched my face. "You're breathing hard, do you need to turn around?"

"How do you do that?" I asked, looking into his comforting blue eyes. "We're talking about something deeply personal to you, and you're still worried about me. You always read my thoughts."

"It's not that hard if you pay attention. We all notice the things we care about."

"Yeah, so what else is on my mind?"

He held steady eye contact as he handed the water bottle back. "You obviously miss LA, you talk about it all the time."

"I do. It's my home. I love it there." An animal rustled in the foliage. I shoved the water into my pack and pushed my foot on the pedal, giving it everything I had.

"It's kind of a superficial place." He pedaled with ease and caught up to me.

"Los Angeles? That's part of its charm." I laughed. "Where else will you meet a woman who got plastic surgery on her feet to please her boyfriend?"

"What? I don't believe that!"

"She's real, she was my mom's friend. It's crazy, right?" My head started to feel dizzy, and I needed to stop again. "I gotta take a break." I stepped off my bicycle and walked it. "I'm sorry I'm so lame. You keep going."

He paced himself by moving up and down beside me. "The air is thinner up here. It can tire you out quicker."

"Oh, good." I rolled my eyes at my own weakness. "I thought it might be that I was completely out of shape. That and I'm feeling the little buzz I get right before I have a panic attack. Don't worry though. If I pay attention and breathe, sometimes I can push it away."

"Did something I say trigger you?"

"No, sometimes they just happen."

"How often?"

I sucked in deeper breaths, trying to force down oxygen as I pushed my bike upwards, struggling against gravity's pull. "Often enough. Meds help, but it's always there. My whole family is the same way. I swear it's like Jew disease. PTSD in our DNA. We're all carrying on the suffering of our ancestors."

"Why'd you pick such a stressful job if you're so anxious all the time?"

"I'm a mess no matter what. Might as well do what I want."

He smiled with enthusiasm. "That's a great attitude."

"It's survival. If I start wussing out on something important because I'm afraid, fear might swallow up my whole life. I'll always do what scares me. It's my motto." My breathing grew shallower. Sweat dripped down my forehead and stung my eyes.

Jack stopped his bike, pulled out a tissue and handed it to me. "Let's turn around. I didn't realize how steep this trail was. We can find a place downtown to get a drink."

"Refreshing." I smiled.

"All right, let's do it." He pointed his front tire downhill and waited for me to do the same.

"Okay," I agreed, "but please go ahead of me. I know you want to fly and I'd rather take it slow."

"You sure?"

"Positive. Go!"

Jack grinned widely before he shot off like an Olympian, his long light-brown legs pumping hard. I squeezed the brakes.

After a small pep-talk, I made myself brave and let go. The wind whooshed past my face, my arms straining against the intense rush of freedom, then I tamped back down.

"Shelbs, hold up," Jack called out, heading back in my direction with a worried look on his face.

"Why'd you turn around? I'm fine."

"Stay right next to me," he demanded. I slammed on my brakes and looked at Jack. His blue eyes focused on the path in between the trees, unwavering and vicious. "There's two guys down the road. One of them's got a pair of crutches and he doesn't need them."

"What do you mean?" I asked, wiping away the dirt sticking to my face.

"I saw them hanging out at the bottom of the trail when we first took off. They were both walking just fine. Now they're hanging out down there, one on each side of the trail. Something's not right."

My mind flashed to the menacing notes taped to my door. The dead rose in my glovebox. Maybe this was a good thing. I could finally confront the predator who'd been stalking me.

"Stay right next to me," he ordered again. "We'll ride down together."

My heart raced with adrenaline. As we rounded a turn, the two men came into view. One, a skinny man with a wifebeater draped over his paper white skin and cheap tattoos. He sat on a rock, holding a metal crutch out at arm's length, the foot of it smashed into the dirt. The second guy was bigger, dreadlocks tied behind a bandanna on his head. The duo looked like homeless thugs.

I slowed my speed, biting hard into my lower lip, no

longer confident Jack and I could take them.

"What do I do?" I spoke barely above a whisper.

"We go," Jack's voice boomed, deep and aggressive.

Every piece of me sensed danger. My vision blurred into slow motion. I could taste the salt on my lips, hear the ringing in my ears. "Do it," my voice demanded. I jerked my foot down harder and pumped fast and furiously.

Dust flew. The men's faces came closer. No smiles. Violent eyes. If anything happened to Jack, it would be my fault. Gnats swarmed my nose and teeth. I kept going. Pushing faster, my lungs burned.

I heard the screech of metal on metal, the crutch jamming through Jack's front wheel spokes. His bike flipped and he skidded face first through the leaves. I stopped.

"Keep going!" Jack yelled.

The bigger man lunged at me. I balled my left hand into a fist and screamed as my knuckles made contact with his face. Bone against bone. I landed a solid punch to his fat nose.

Blood ran red. Years of boxing lessons and fist fights as a teenager had prepared me. The man reached for my neck. I tried to get into a grounded position, but I couldn't get off my bike fast enough. I leaned back and fell, my bike tangled on top of me.

My body shook with rage. I levied myself on my elbows, powering back in the leaves the way my dad's trainer had taught me. I kicked the bike at the man's feet, preparing for a fight.

"You can't report the news if your face is smashed in, stupid bitch." He lurched over the bike, leaning over and grabbing my ankle, yanking me forward through the leaves and dirt. "I've been watching you. I know where you live. Still wanna act tough, Shelby Day?"

My nerves shot off like a bomb. Fear vibrated all the way down my legs to my feet. He knew me. It had to be him. My stalker. He was the person who'd been threatening me. He could also be a murderer.

My vision narrowed. All I could see was the glint of madness in his dilated black eyes. The man reached down to grab me. I blasted my foot as hard as I could into his crotch.

He dropped to his knees and held himself, his bandanna coming loose, dreadlocks falling into his face. "Whore," he seethed. The man reached out and snatched my leg, putting his elbow on my arm, pinning me down, so I couldn't escape. He took hold of my other arm, ripping the ring off my finger. I lunged forward, grabbing his dreadlocks and yanking them far back. He pushed his arm across my face, seizing my elbow. My opportunity was there. I bit into his fat wrist. Tendons and bones. I tasted blood in my mouth. His blood.

He yanked his hand from my mouth, blood pouring down my chin. I huffed in triumph, but his hand came back at me again, this time in a fist. I could hear Jack yelling for me, fear and rage colliding on his soft lips. But it was too late, I'd already lost.

CHAPTER TWELVE

I regained consciousness staring into Jack's concerned eyes. The crook of his arm supported my head, my body cradled in the warmth of his lap like a sleeping child.

"Shelbs, are you okay? An ambulance is coming."

Sirens blared in the near distance. "Paramedics?" Turning my head slowly to look around, I saw the blurred outlines of several police officers restraining the two men who had assaulted us.

My vision became clearer. Strangers in jeans and sweatshirts stood in the parking lot directly below the trail head, watching us. I flashed back to the powerful fist that had slammed my cheek and then the quiet. Blackout.

Touching my face, I winced at the sharp pain. "No ambulance." I looked back up at Jack. "Your face is bruised," I said to him, "and your lips are swollen. Jack, I'm so sorry. This is all my fault."

He gave me a tight smile. Tears welled in his eyes. "I'm fine, Shelby. None of this is your fault. All that matters is that you're awake."

"Hi, Shelby." Another familiar face came into view. A

tall man with a bald head squatted down closer to my level. "Do you know who I am?"

"Sergeant Dunbar." My thoughts came into sharper focus. "I was going to call you tomorrow to ask you some questions about the murders on Belle Street."

He chuckled, pulling a flashlight from his belt and flashing it in my eyes. He asked me questions about the year and what I was doing. I answered them but pushed harder on the Belle street murders. "Always work with you, Shelby Day? We can talk about this later. Right now I want to make sure you're safe. Can you tell me what happened?"

I sat up with care and gently scooched off Jack's lap, placing myself right next to him at the bottom of the trail. Disorientated, I squinted into the setting sun, the sky a burst of orange. The back of my head pounded and my entire body ached. I pressed my hand to my right cheek once again and worried if Jack was really okay.

He kept his hand on my lap, squeezing the top of my thigh with protective concern. I placed my hand over his and squeezed him back.

"They ambushed us," I told Sergeant Dunbar, flinching at the memory. "One of the guys knocked out Jack's bike with a crutch and the other one punched me in the face."

"Do you mind if I take some pictures of your wounds for evidence?"

"Sure." I pushed up my sleeves and held out my arms. "What happened after I blacked out?" I asked Jack as the Sergeant snapped pictures.

"Nothing ha—"

"Well, it looks like he broke the first man's arm. Too bad

he had crutches and not a cast." Sergeant Dunbar chuckled into his camera.

"But what happened to the guy on top of me?" I asked.

"I kicked him in the face," Jack said, his blue eyes gone dark, as he traced the movements of the men now restrained in the back of the police cars. The bigger one with dreadlocks sported a black eye with a face-full of blood. When he saw Jack's gaze he looked away.

There was no doubt the man in dreadlocks was my stalker, and now he'd gotten physical and come after me. Who knew what he would've done if Jack hadn't been able to stop him? No one was safe with a villain like that free to strike again.

Sergeant Dunbar continued snapping pictures of me while Jack took over telling me the story. "Two other cyclists came up the trail. They saw what was going on and helped me out. One of them called 911."

"Heroes," I said, stunned that any of this was real. "I need to thank them in person."

"Certainly." Sergeant Dunbar put away his cell and rubbed the top of his head. "The situation could have escalated and become a whole lot worse. Shelby, are you missing anything?"

Jack shook his head, "They didn't try to take anything from me."

My gaze ping-ponged between Jack and Sergeant Dunbar, as if they held the answer. Then my gaze drifted down to my right hand. Something was missing. "The guy with dreadlocks. The one who punched me. He ripped my grandmother's wedding ring off my finger before he hit me. It was a sapphire, like Princess Diana's, only smaller."

Tears formed in my eyes, hot as they fell down my cold cheeks. My baba had given the ring to me when I turned sixteen. She said she wanted me to have it because she knew how much I loved it. It was originally my great-grandmother's. She wanted to be around to see me enjoy wearing her mom's most treasured piece of jewelry.

"We have to get it back from him." I averted my gaze to my bruised hand. Rubbing my finger, I remembered what my ring felt like, the weight and security of it.

Distant sirens grew louder and came to an abrupt stop. Paramedics had arrived.

"Did he take anything else that you know of?" Sergeant Dunbar asked.

I shrugged my shoulders. "I don't think so. That was all that mattered anyway. Did one of you already find it on him? He had to have stuck in his pocket or something."

Sergeant Dunbar looked over at the ambulance as two men exited the vehicle. "We'll do a search at the station."

The dying sun sank lower on the horizon, casting deep shadows over the Siskiyou Mountains. I dug at the dirt wedged beneath my fingernails as the breeze picked up and layered my skin in goosebumps. *Why did they have to wait until they got to the station?*

I tried to stand but felt too woozy for the task. Jack helped me settle back down beside him. I glanced over again at Sergeant Dunbar. "There's something important I need to tell you."

He pulled out a notebook and a pen from his shirt's front pocket. My eyes traveled down the holster attached to his thick brown belt, a gun fastened inside decorated his hip.

"My attacker knew my name. He said he'd been watching

me and he knew I was on television. Somebody's been leaving typed notes on my front door telling me to stop covering the murder investigation—I mean, they never said that specifically, but they said to stop reporting the story. Do you think the dreadlocked guy could be the killer?"

Sergeant Dunbar rubbed his index finger across his thick mustache, a look of concern in his troubled brown eyes. "We'll take a swab for DNA, but we can't be certain that they're connected right now. Be assured, Shelby, we'll look into it."

"Why didn't you tell me any of this?" Jack said, a sharp look of hurt pained across his face. "I would have stayed over at your house to make sure you're safe."

Before I could speak, two paramedics approached. I did my best to wave them off. "I'm fine, take a look at him." I pointed to Jack.

"I'm good, man." Jack dusted off his legs. "Just some scrapes and bruises."

The older of the two guys, a muscular blond somewhere in his late twenties with dimpled cheeks, put his hands on his hips. "How many times did you get hit?" he asked me.

As if reliving the experience, I wiped at my lips, noticing the metallic taste of blood in my mouth. "Only once, in the face. I've been knocked out before, I'm okay."

"What did he hit you with?"

"His fist. I'm fine, really."

"Ma'am, you understand that if you refuse transport you are doing so against medical advice. You have a right to do so, but if you were knocked unconscious you should see a doctor. You have cuts on your face. If you'd let me, I'd like to dress your wounds."

"Do you see anything on my face that could leave a scar?" I asked, feeling a tightening in my gut. If people complained about my thin eyebrows, imagine what they might say about permanent marks on my face.

He looked me over. "Can't say for sure. Probably not."

"I'm good, then. I've been knocked out before, I know how to look for a concussion. If I need to see a doctor, I can go on my own."

The dimpled paramedic kicked at the dirt. "I can't force either of you, but I'd go see your doctors so they can take you in for X-rays or an MRI. You could have internal wounds that aren't obvious yet."

"Thanks," I said on behalf of both Jack and me.

Dimples looked at Sergeant Dunbar. "Is there anyone else you need us to look at?"

"Yes, the two other men over there with the bikes." He lifted his chin toward the fit weekend warriors typing on their cell phones. "They also were involved with the assailants."

"Will do. Thanks guys." Dimples nodded at me. "I hope you're okay."

"Thanks." I shielded my eyes from the glare of the setting sun.

"What are you going to do about the notes?" Jack asked Sergeant Dunbar.

"Unfortunately, there's not much we can do." The Sergeant looked at me. "I recommend, if you're uncomfortable, you invest in a good lock and get some security cameras to secure your home. You can get one online for a few bucks that will give you notifications when somebody's out front. This way you can identify the suspect and call the police if somebody's on your property. If it happens again, document the notes on the door with photographs and dates, that way, if they become overtly threating, we'll have a chance at identifying the person."

Jack's eyes opened wider in disbelief. "That's it?"

"If I could do something more, I would." Sergeant Dunbar pursed his lips together. "But, there's not much I can do about it at this point. If the man who attacked you is the same person leaving those notes, he should be going away for a while. But it's better to take precautions."

I looked over at both men. "I'm not worried about it happening again, because I'm telling you right now, I'm positive that creep your guys hauled off is my stalker. I just want to make sure he's going to jail."

"They should be put away even longer for stalking." Jack's jaw clenched.

Sergeant Dunbar frowned. "It's not illegal to post notes on somebody's front door. Assault, battery, robbery, those are things we can work with."

"That's probably for the best." I hunched forward, enough to create some protective space from Jack and the Sergeant. "I don't want anything about those notes getting out to the media, anyway. Management would probably find a way to fire me if they thought I was a liability. If my mom found out, I'd never hear the end of it." My mother would insist I move home, marry a nice Jewish boy, and hole up inside our gated fortress twenty-four-seven for the rest of my life. I'd rather die.

No sooner did I think the worst was over when Becca Barnes with her frizzy hair and a news camera slung over her shoulder came trudging up toward the trail. "Oh, my gosh," she called out with concern, her wide-eyes completely focused on Jack. "Are you guys all right?"

She must have heard about the incident on the police scanners. I pulled my phone out of my thrashed little backpack and sure enough I had a slew of missed texts and phone calls from our assignment desk.

"Sergeant Dunbar." I pushed up at my right sleeve. "Promise me the media won't hear about the notes."

"Notes? What notes?" Sergeant Dunbar grinned before standing to speak with Becca Barnes, asking her to step away to give Jack and me space to breathe. I liked Dunbar.

"We need to get you a taser," Jack said.

"I'd rather have a gun like the one the Sergeant's carrying."

"This is serious, Shelby." Jack pinched his lips together.

I could feel my muscles tighten in response. "Okay, Mr. Peace, Love, surfer-guy. You've got something against guns?"

"I don't. I grew up around them and I know how to use them."

"Well, I can learn."

He rubbed his hand against his toned leg. "I'm pretty sure you can't carry a gun to work. But we might be able to get you a concealed carry permit."

Regardless of what he came up with, I was finished with playing the role of the victim.

CHAPTER THIRTEEN

Even without footage of us beaten and bruised, Becca Barnes managed to capture plenty of other shots for her story, including the police cars, the ambulance, and of course, a sound bite from the dimpled paramedic. We were lucky Sergeant Dunbar managed to shoo her away before she snagged any video of Jack or me splayed out on the dirt path.

Still, there was no way around it, I was going to be interviewed. But there was zero chance I'd let somebody like Becca Barnes do it. Begrudgingly, Jack and I gave Lily Park an exclusive back at the station.

She put together her own competing story for *NBC 4* on the alleged violent robbery that occurred on an Alice in Wonderland Trail. After following up with the police, Lily discovered both of our attackers were local vagrants with minor criminal records. The police couldn't find my grandmother's ring.

Lily did, however, assure me the men were going to be kept in custody until their arraignment on Monday or Tuesday, and that the police were collecting DNA samples to determine if either of the men were a match for Melissa and Daphne's killer.

As I walked off the set from our live interview, I wrung my hands. The owner of the news station, Georgia McAllaster, a sturdy petite blonde in her mid-fifties, stood waiting for me, her eyes knitted with concern.

"Shelby, how are you?" Georgia pushed her hair behind her ear, her intense eyes searching my face, wincing at the bruises.

"I'm feeling pretty well, really." My right hand involuntarily stroked my swollen cheek. "I'll apply thicker makeup to cover up anything on camera. No one will notice."

"Oh, I'm not worried about that. I'm worried about you. I already told Jack, you both need to take at least a few days off work." She shook her head. "What a terrifying experience."

I tugged at the pink beaded bracelet Jack had given me. Time off felt like a punishment. "They were just some thugs looking for our spare change. I'm totally fine, I don't need time off."

"I spoke with the police department," Georgia said, ignoring my plea to keep me on the schedule. "The merchants downtown have been ramping up pressure to have something done about the homeless population at Lithia park as well as up and down Main Street."

"It's about time." I knew the restaurant and shop owners were sick of the loitering in front of their businesses. Unfortunately, our locals were more worried about police brutality than public safety.

Georgia pressed her hands into a steeple. "Yes, well, what with the murders on Belle Street, officers will have the public's support to step in and do something. What happened to you and Jack is really going to push things over the top." She placed her hand on my shoulder. "The watch commander told me they're organizing a town meeting by the end of this week. This shouldn't ever be an issue for you again. Your poor parents must be worried sick."

I bit at my lower lip, anxiety churning in my belly at the mention of Mom and Dad. With my mom's constant watch, I was surprised that she hadn't already seen the news story on Facebook and called me, nagging me to come home. She must be distracted by Dad's illness.

"Georgia..." I cursed the nerves bubbling in my gut, "I'm glad to hear folks around here are finally taking these people seriously. Yeah, they look like hippies and try to pass themselves off as harmless, but they're neither. It's more obvious than ever, they're dangerous."

I prepared my argument in my head, building confidence. "Besides, I'm feeling good. I beat the heck out of that guy and it was empowering. I'd love to cover the town hall meeting, it's the perfect new angle on the murders and I'm the lead on that story. Plus, I can't really afford to take time off work, I have rent to make."

Doors flew open behind me and the shadow of a person shot inside the room. I winced, anxiety painting possibilities of the dreadlock man returning to finish me off. My nerves calmed when the shape of the production assistant formed.

Georgia gave me a curt nod. "The town hall meeting is probably going to be held before you return from your time off. Your *paid* time off. Shelby, you sleep and take care of yourself. Let us know if you need anything. We'll look out for you, we're like family here. And don't worry, we'll all be waiting for you with open arms when you return."

I nodded in defeat. Georgia gave me a quick hug and excused herself, heading off toward the control room. Jack wasted no time waving me over to his desk. "Hey, Shelbs, come check this out." He lifted his chin toward his computer.

Harsh fluorescent lights in the empty newsroom emphasized the sweaty welts and glistening bumps covering his face. I couldn't help but feel responsible for his injuries. I knew I shouldn't have taken him up on his offer on the bikes. If I'd followed my gut, none of this would've happened.

"What's wrong?" he asked.

"Nothing. What's up?"

"Why do you want to stay at the station? You've earned the sick leave, Shelbs."

My stomach churned and I could feel a tightening in my chest. "There's no reason to leave. Everything's handled."

"Check this out," he spoke in hushed excitement. "It's cool if I stick with you for a while, keep an eye on you, make sure you're safe. I've been googling stun guns and tasers and I think that tasers are definitely the way to go, way—."

"More powerful." I finished Jack's sentence. I'd done more than my fair share of research already. Even though I was certain my note-writing, dead-rose-leaving, face-punching attacker had been captured, getting beat up today made it clear, I needed protection. You never knew when someone was going to go on the attack. "I'd rather have a gun," I spoke in a hushed tone, not wanting anyone to overhear our conversation echoing in the hollow building. "A gun seems more effective."

Jack pointed to the picture on the screen. "This will keep you just as safe. Check it out, it's the same one the police use. It's a stun gun and a taser in one, you can put it directly against somebody or it'll shoot out two probe darts. You don't need to touch anyone. Or have anyone touch you. Just like a gun."

The picture on the computer showed an intimidating black weapon with a pistol grip and a long square barrel that housed a laser pointer hanging underneath it. "It looks like a real gun."

"Well, not really. To you, maybe." The screen went dark and he had to wiggle the mouse to make it light back up. "But this way, you can't get fired for taking a gun to work."

"That's a good selling point."

Jack smiled at the screen with excitement. "As long you keep your finger on the trigger, you're going to be juicing your target up with electricity. Fifty thousand volts. That sucker won't be able to move."

"What happens when I let go?"

"His muscles will stop contracting and after he recovers, he'll be able to stand up. Doesn't mean he'd want to, though."

I could picture the scene in my head. An outlaw steps out of the shadows and *boom*, I blast him with my taser. With my free hand, I'd call 911. "It's perfect." I smiled.

"You have to pass a felony background check before they ship it. I'm going to order one now and hopefully it won't take more than a few days. I'll pay extra for overnight shipping."

"Are you kidding me?" I scanned the screen for pricing. "It's almost eight hundred dollars. That's too much."

"Not for your protection, it's not."

He was already doting on me, like my dad with my mom. Maybe this budding relationship wasn't a good idea, after all.

"Jack, that's way too much, I can't accept that."

"You forget, I do tech support around here, and I run the live truck. I can afford it." He flashed me his movie-star smile. "Besides, I'll put it on my credit card. Don't worry about it."

"I don't know."

"I just want to make sure you're safe." He cocked his head to the side, admiring me. "You're my girl, after all."

His *girl*? I pulled my hair back into a messy bun, feeling overheated. I couldn't bear to break his heart, but I didn't know if I could be his girl. Really, I didn't even know what I wanted. Was settling down into the monotony of a relationship something that I could even do? Or would I sabotage it like I always did? "I'm not your girl, Jack."

"What do you mean?" He flinched as if I'd reached out to slap him. "What are you to me?"

"I don't know yet," I told him the truth. "I really like you, Jack, but I feel like we're rushing things."

"You got attacked today, Shelby." He rolled his chair out from under the desk. "Whatever we are, I want to protect you."

"Jack, you're blowing this out of proportion. I'll be fine. And, as far as dating goes, we only kissed; it's not like you're my boyfriend or anything."

"You're not seeing anyone else, are you?"

"Would that be so terrible?" I flayed my hands out on the table. It'd been one day. We weren't exclusive. Even though I cared for Jack, I could still date who I wanted.

Hurt flashed in his blue eyes. How would you feel if I went out with Becca Barnes, or hooked up with Kaya again?"

"Again?" I could feel my stomach tie into a knot.

"That's not the point."

"Then what is the point?" I spat, defensiveness souring my tone.

Jack looked into my eyes and softened his voice. "Shelby, if we're going to see each other, it needs to be exclusive. I'm not into open relationships."

"I just need some time to feel comfortable, that's all." I chewed on my thumbnail, my defenses lowering. "It's kind of been a long day anyway, don't you think?"

"If you need time Shelbs, that's cool. I'll wait as long as you need." Jack ran his hand through his dark hair. "But either way, I'd still like to order the taser. Once all of this is over with, I can sell it or give it to my cousin. This way I won't be out the money. Does that work?"

"Yes." I was happy Jack was giving me some time to get more comfortable with our relationship.

"I also think I should sleep on your couch until the taser gets here."

I crossed my arms over my chest. Why couldn't he understand that giving me time also meant giving me my space? "Those men are behind bars until at least tomorrow. I'm safer than I've been in weeks." I puffed my chest out, trying to act bigger than I was.

Jack shook his head. "It doesn't make sense. If your stalker wanted to hurt you, why'd he bother taking the time to steal from you?" His face went slack. "I'm so sorry they got your ring. It was beautiful."

"You saw it? I didn't think you'd have noticed." I rubbed my blackened and bruised finger. "I didn't wear my baba's ring all the time. It's kind of weird I wore it today at all, seeing as we were going biking."

"I notice everything about you." He looked at me with affection.

"I don't know how the police didn't find it, but maybe it'll still show up," I said, trying to be positive. "I'm just happy you didn't get too hurt. I'd never forgive myself if you had something permanent happen because of me. Thank you for what you did today."

"It was nothing." He nodded, seeming lost in his thoughts.

"Look," I tried to reassure him, "there's no doubt he's the one who was stalking me."

"But how do you know that? Any good friend would want to look out for you right now, Shelby. We're all stronger when we have someone who's got our back." His eyes pleaded with me to say yes.

My heart softened. I didn't have the strength to continue resisting him, not tonight. "If it's so important to you, we can stay at your apartment."

I inhaled, feeling the knot pull tighter in my stomach. After such an intense day, I knew myself well enough to know this; once I stepped through Jack's front door, it was going to be very hard to stay on the couch.

CHAPTER FOURTEEN

I needed space, I needed time, but tossing and turning in his cold empty bed, the only thing I could think about was how badly I wanted Jack.

Shimmering moonlight guided me as I crept into the living room and sat beside him on the frayed checkerboard couch where he lay. "Jack," I whispered. "Jack, are you awake?"

His eyes blinked in the moonlit room.

"Jack?" I traced my fingers along his arm. "Come to bed with me. Please?"

"Shelbs." He ran his hand through his hair in frustration. "Come on."

"I don't want to be alone," I said, determined to win him over. "Can't we just cuddle?"

"Cuddle?" Jack groaned, a hint of sarcasm texturing his tired voice. "*Sure.*"

"Come on," I smiled, tugging gently at his arm. "I promise I won't let you do anything you'll regret in the morning."

He squeezed the top of my hand with a chuckle and gathered his pillow to follow me back to his room. Snuggled into his bed under warm blankets, I turned to face him. "Thank you for everything you did today."

He touched his hand to my cheek. "I was only looking out for who I care about."

"You have to admit, I kicked that guy's ass. I mean, until his fist came at my face." My lips quivered as my body finally let go, safe to feel vulnerable. "That was honestly the scariest thing that's ever happened to me."

Jack's arms tightened around my waist, pulling me in close as I rested my cheek on his chest. The warmth and comfort of his embrace felt better than the best massage, peeling off skinny jeans, or flipping over my pillow on a hot night.

"I don't want you to worry, Shelby. When I'm around, I'll do everything in my power to keep you safe."

I tilted my chin up, inhaling the scent of him. Instinctively, I pressed in even closer, and could feel he wanted me as much as I wanted him.

With an intake of air, his lips found my lips. My fingers dug into his broad back. My hands on his body, his hands all over mine. Every piece of me craved more of him. We stayed that way, touching, kissing, crashing along the edges of desire, until he slowly pulled away.

"We can't do this, Shelby."

"I can't just kiss you?" I teased, pressing in to brush my lips against his once more.

He drew his head back just out of reach. "I don't want you to sleep with me just because I'm here and you're coming off the adrenaline of what happened today. I care about you, Shelby, a lot. I don't want to screw this up."

My primal instincts screamed for that rush of endorphins

and momentary suspension of time and place, but wiser pieces of me agreed with Jack. I adored my best friend. He was the ideal man; handsome, kind, and always looking out for my best interests. My heart begged to give all of myself to him, to fall so deeply I'd give everything I had to be together.

But I knew the truth. I wasn't capable of that kind of love. I'd find a way to ruin it.

"You're right, Jack." Using every bit of my emotional strength, I flipped over, pressed my back against his firm chest and took cleansing breaths to calm my pulse. "I kind of hate you right now, though, for turning me on so much."

"I kind of hate myself right now too." His lips swept against my ear.

I smiled just a little, secretly relieved he was as tortured as I was. Snuggling deep into my pillow, I closed my eyes and allowed my body to drift asleep.

—

Morning light feathered the blinds, turning Jack's Downy-scented black sheets a soft dusty shade of gray.

"Good morning, beautiful." His deep hum woke me late in the morning.

Even in my fuzzy state, I tried to wipe the sleep from my eyes before Jack could get a good look at me.

"You hungry?" he asked.

"I can cook," I said. "Do you have eggs and cheese? My omelets are epic."

"I don't have anything." He pulled me in and kissed the top of my head. "That's why it's better if tonight we stay at your place."

"We can talk about that later." I reached out and checked my cell for the time before cuddling back into him. He'd turned me down last night and yet he was already trying to get me to spend the night with him again. I felt more confused than I imagined possible.

Ignoring my angst, I looked up at him. The bruises on his left cheek and chin had seeped a deep purple. "How are you feeling? Those look like they hurt."

"It was worth it. I was protecting you."

"Jack, be serious."

"I am." He swept the bangs from my eyes and smiled. "Brown-eyed girl."

"Want to trade?" I chuckled. "I'll take your awesome blue eyes, you can have my boring brown ones."

"No thanks, I like you exactly the way you are." He tousled my hair. "You got a bunch of texts last night after you passed out."

"Probably from my mom."

"You think it's anything serious?" he asked.

"I don't know."

"Could it be about your dad? You've barely said another word about him since you told me he was sick."

"Do you ever smoke inside?" I asked, pushing up into a sitting position, feeling uncomfortable at the mention of my dad's health.

"Sure. There's no way we're getting our security deposit back, anyway. My roommate's a disaster." He reached into his end-table and pulled out a pack of American Spirits along with a green plastic lighter. I watched as he placed a cigarette in his mouth, lighting it. He took a quick puff and handed it to me.

I wrapped my lips around the cigarette for a long drag. Nicotine pulsed through my veins and eased the anxiety.

"Need a glass for the ashes?" Jack pointed to an empty one near his side of the bed.

"Thanks." I took another pull and blew the blue-white plume of smoke away from Jack's face. "I don't like talking about my dad when I'm sober."

"Okay," he said, keeping the expression on his face blank.

I handed him the cigarette and watched him flip the ash into the glass before taking a pull. I prepared to open up to Jack, to say the dreaded c-word out loud again, as if the word held dark magic that might make Dad's illness more real.

My words came out clipped at first, forced, like pulling poison from a wound. "Prostate cancer. I'm fucking terrified. The surgery's today. I can't even think about it. What if something goes sideways? What if the doctors got it wrong and it's actually already started spreading throughout his body? I've always had a screwy relationship with my parents, but I love them more than anything in this world. I'd give my dad my own prostate if I had one. My parents are my center."

"I think a lot of people feel that way about their family." He squeezed my free hand. "Maybe you should check your messages, make sure everything's all right."

"I called my dad last night before we left the newsroom and wished him luck. Nothing's happened between then and now. My mom's just freaking out."

"Makes sense."

"It's only stage one," I said, trying hard to stuff down all the heavy emotion. "The operation will go smoothly and this whole ugly thing will be over with." I pushed my thumb against the splotchy purple and green bruise near my shoulder, relishing in the pain. "Can we change the subject, please?"

"Sure. What do you want to talk about?"

"Tit for tat?" I asked, wondering once again about Jack's secret. "It's only fair."

Jack slid back down to lie on his back, his right hand holding firm to the cigarette. "I've told you everything."

"That's not true, Jack Miller. I've been your friend for what, almost a year now? And you still haven't told me why you left San Diego."

"It's not a pretty story, Shelby," he said, his voice filling with tension.

"Neither is prostate cancer."

He passed me the cigarette and dragged his hand down his face.

"All right, I warned you."

"I appreciate that, Jack."

He inhaled deeply though his nose and exhaled. "Elaine was my girlfriend for seven years. I met her in the seventh grade and we were together ever since."

"Yeah?" I took a puff on the cigarette, wondering what Elaine was like.

"She was the sweetest girl you could ever meet. Really. She never complained about anything. She'd wait all day on the beach for me to get out of the water. She asked me to teach her to surf, but I never did, and she just let it go. That's how she was. She never gave me a hard time about anything really, hung out with all my friends. Everyone loved her, my mom, my buddies . . ."

"Your first love." I said, my words spiked with the tinge

of envy. Not because he'd felt that way about another girl, but because of those feelings. Feelings I'd never fully allowed myself to experience.

Jack's nostrils flared and his eyes burned with regret.

"What happened?" I asked.

His jaw pulsed.

"You cheated on her," I said, certain of the answer.

"Everything came so easy. When Elaine wasn't around, other girls came at me. I was too dumb to realize I was hurting her." He removed his hand from his face and reached for the cigarette, taking a puff before he continued.

"I'm sure she heard whispers, but she never said anything. I broke up with a her a couple of times because I felt guilty, but then she would show up wherever I was, looking so pretty, with her long brown hair and sweet blue eyes, and we'd end up back together."

My tummy ached for this poor girl. Nothing hurt like not being loved back.

Jack continued, "After high school, we got an apartment. She went to college and worked part-time as a waitress, and I wasted my days. Smoking weed. Surfing. Being an idiot. I met a girl who paid a lot of attention to me and sure enough, I cheated on Elaine again. When I told her I wanted to break up, she told me that if this was it, then it was it, she wouldn't take me back again."

"And?"

"I packed my bags." Jack tugged at the comforter and smoothed it out across his chest. "Moved in with my new girl, Nika, and her roommates. Two months later, I found out Nika was hooking up with some other guy. I finally got it. I knew how it felt to be betrayed. It changed me."

"And when you tried to win back Elaine, she gave you the cold shoulder so you moved to Ashland?"

He pinched his bottom lip. "I begged her for another chance. I even set up a shrine to her in my bedroom at my parents'. One night, I threatened to stab myself with a pencil if she didn't take me back. I still have the scar. Total jerk. Once she got a new boyfriend, I started to move on. I still wasn't over her, but he treated her right, better than I did. Then one day they went out surfing together and she got smashed by her board. She ended up in the hospital with a compound fracture in her leg. I don't know exactly what happened. The doctors said she could go home in the morning. But the next morning she was dead."

"What?" I shot up straighter. "Why? How old was she?"

"Nineteen." He wiped at his watering eyes. "I don't know why, it was maybe some sort of fast-moving infection, a hematoma, I don't know. Nobody would tell me. Nobody wanted to tell me. I just, if I'd been there for her, you know? If I was more loyal in the first place, if I'd tried harder to get her back, or if I even took her out to surf with me once and a while, taught her the basics, she'd probably still be here."

I squeezed his arm. "You don't know that. What happened to Elaine wasn't your fault, Jack. It was a freak accident."

"And then my mom died." A tear slipped down his face, but his voice was unbroken. "All in a matter of months. The world lost two of the best women I'll ever know."

"Jack, I'm so sorry." I felt his anguish. "You're so strong for going through that. Nobody should have to experience so much loss. Especially not all at once."

He stared at the ceiling. "They led me here, my mom and Elaine. My mom's looking out for me."

I snuggled down into him and rubbed my index finger across his wet cheek. "Your mom would be so proud of how much you've accomplished, and how you treat others. She raised a good son."

He took the dying cigarette from my hand and stubbed it out in the glass. "She would've loved you."

"Do you really think so?"

"Of course. Why wouldn't she?"

"Jack," I asked, almost afraid to ask my next question, "why do you even like me? You said so yourself, Elaine was the sweetest girl you ever met. With me, most guys write me off as a pain in the ass. I kind of annoy myself half the time."

"You?" He looked at me with mock surprise and tickled my waist.

"Yeah, I know it's hard to believe." I fought the urge to roll my eyes as I scooched away from his tickles.

Jack reached out and wrapped his pinkie finger around mine. "I've never met anybody like you before, Shelby. In a good way. You challenge me, hardcore. You make me feel alive."

He tucked a strand of my hair behind my ear. "You're so smart, and passionate about everything you do. I love how driven you are, how you make me think, how you make me want to be better. You're also an awesome friend, even when you're messing with me."

My lips twisted in concern. "So then, why did you call me a Lost Girl?"

Jack chuckled. "You're not going to forget that are you?"

"No."

"No one's perfect, Shelby. I don't want you to change who you are. I only meant we all need balance. You get so caught up in showing the world you're more than where you came from. You forget that our families and our circumstances make up only a piece of who we are. I watch you get so lost in your career, Shelbs, trying to prove your worth, you miss out on some of the great stuff. The stuff that makes life worth living."

"Hmmm . . ." I rolled over onto my back and considered his observations.

"Every day I look at you through the camera, and when I see your face with that beautiful smile, I love the things that you do and what you say. I can't help but feel like I need to be near you. You make me a better person, Shelby. I like who I am when I'm with you."

I took in all his words, rolling them around in my head, pondering if everything he said could be true.

"Come on." He gave me a gentle nudge. "Quit over-analyzing. Let's get out of here and eat some breakfast."

I leaned onto my elbow and ran my fingers over the soft sheet. "I'd love to. If you want, you can tell me more stories about Elaine and your mom. Sometimes it's good to talk, it helps keep them alive."

"Let's do it. Where do you want to go?"

"Waffle Barn. Lots of butter, crispy bacon. Coffee. Then afterwards, don't make fun of me, but I have a little work to get done today."

"We have the next few days off."

"I still need to talk to a couple of people. Like Sergeant Dunbar. The arraignment for the two losers who attacked us might be today, and I have a few questions I want to follow up with about Daphne DeLuca and Melissa Rossi." It was important to keep focused on the investigation before my personal life swept away essential obligations.

"It's Sunday, Shelbs."

I wrinkled my nose at him.

He leaned in closer. "Don't you remember you're supposed to be recuperating? If it were up to those paramedics, you'd be in the hospital right now, all strung out on pain meds and getting X-rays and examinations. What can I do to convince you to relax a little longer?"

I inhaled, tempted to let go, to take advantage of the luxury of his embrace.

His eyes fixed on mine. "I really like spending time with you." Jack delicately kissed the scrapes and bruises on my face, before he moved to my lips. The heater whirred on and blew a warm breeze across my shoulder blades.

Despite my plan to protect my heart, Jack was slowly winning me over. And that scared me. A lot.

CHAPTER FIFTEEN

Later that afternoon, I moved myself back and forth in the chair placed before Sergeant Dunbar's desk. "This isn't how I imagined the inside of a small-town police station." I took in the gleaming glass skylights, modern Shaker-style furniture, and shiny new Apple laptops. It smelled like fresh carpet.

"They renovated the interior a few years back, it's the nicest station in Oregon." The length of his long torso puffed with pride. "You're here about the arraignment?"

"How'd it go?" I asked, feeling a little guilty I'd ditched Jack so I could come alone. This news affected him, too.

"The judge charged them both with aggravated assault and felony armed robbery."

"Why armed robbery? They didn't have a gun or knives or anything, did they?" I could feel my limbs tingle with fear.

"The crutch," he said, taking a swig from his Ashland PD coffee mug, stained from use. I could almost smell the sugar and cream. "That counts as a weapon."

"Makes sense," I murmured, worrying once again about

my grandmother's ring. I reminded myself, it was her way of looking out for me. A stolen ring meant an extended sentence, which gave me more time in Ashland before those thugs were free to hunt me down again.

"Judge Santos set bail at one hundred thousand each. A preliminary trial date was confirmed for mid-November."

I tapped my nervous fingers on his desk. "Is anyone going to bail them out?"

"Unlikely. Both men are indigent and they're using state-assigned attorneys. We'll let you know if they make bail, but otherwise, assume these guys are off the streets for at least another two weeks."

I picked at the chipped, pale pink nail polish coating my thumb. "You still don't think those guys had anything to do with the murders on Belle Street?"

"We gathered saliva swabs and took blood samples. If there's a match, we'll know in a few weeks. The killer was hurt during the attack, he left drops of his blood on the floor and on the windowsill as he was escaping. We've got crucial DNA evidence."

"It's been almost two weeks since the murders. Any other new leads? Anything you can share?"

Sergeant Dunbar frowned. "Those murders weren't a random attack. We're fairly certain the killer knew Daphne or Melissa, or possibly both of them."

Before questioning him any further, I grabbed my cell, "Do you mind if I record this?"

"Aren't you supposed to be taking some time off?" Sergeant Dunbar chuckled, "That's what your colleague who interviewed me yesterday said, anyway. Asian girl? Long black hair."

I clenched my jaw at the thought of Lily Park stealing my lead story. There was no way I would allow that to happen. "I'm here for my own peace of mind. But if we're talking, might as well get the latest info on tape."

I fiddled with my phone. "Everyone I meet is terrified. Nothing like this has ever happened in Ashland before. No one's going to feel safe until the killer's caught, and the more information that's out there, the more leads you'll get. Somebody knows something." I licked my lips like a cat stalking a sparrow.

Dunbar placed his long hands behind his head and leaned back in his weathered high-back office chair, no doubt a relic from before the police station underwent renovations. "Go ahead. I'm not the one who told you to take time off work. Did you ever go get looked at, by the way?"

Without thinking, I touched my cheek, caressing the bruise I'd tried to bury under foundation and powdered blush. "I think I'm fine." I tapped the red record button on my cell phone. "Okay, Sergeant Dunbar, we're recording. Can you tell me why you suspect the killer on Belle Street knew his victims?"

"The assailant walked straight to the stairs once he entered the residence. The surviving roommate heard footsteps walking directly toward the two girls' bedrooms. He knew exactly where he was going and where the girls slept."

"And the crime scene: any new theories?"

"The locations of the blood tell a story. It tells us where the women were when they were attacked, and the manner in which they fought back. Wounds on Daphne's body suggest she was the intended target. Or at the very least it tells us that she was the killer's first victim. We think that she was assaulted while she was sleeping but woke up and attempted to escape. Our best guess right now is that she ran to Melissa's room for help and Melissa tried to save her."

"Interesting, so you're sure Daphne was attacked first?" I asked.

"Nothing is concrete, but the evidence indicates something like that happened."

I felt protective of Daphne and her mother, and I resented that folks in town seemed to blame Daphne for the murders. His theory didn't make sense to me. "Did you find blood in Daphne's bed?" I asked, searching for a new angle. "Maybe she went into Melissa's room because she heard Melissa screaming and she wanted to help her."

"It's conceivable." He placed his hands on his desk. "There are a number of possibilities."

I made a mental note to use that quote in the story I planned to post on social media. "And you can confirm that the third roommate stayed downstairs while the murders took place?"

"Correct. She heard noises and was scared. She hid downstairs until she heard the attacker leave the premises."

"What's next in the investigation?" I asked, not wanting to lose momentum.

Sergeant Dunbar tugged at his mustache. "Outside of the people of interest in Melissa's life, Daphne dated many different men in the short time she lived here. That opens up a large pool of potential suspects. We're talking to every man she dated or had relations with and are testing their DNA to see if they're a match with the killer's DNA."

"How's that going?" I asked.

"It's tedious work. We're eleven days out from the crime and we've already interviewed and collected DNA samples from dozens of potential suspects. We started with the girls' inner circle, people who knew the victims, all of Daphne's boyfriends, Melissa's boyfriend, all of the girls' friends and friends of friends. We're ruling them out as suspects one by one."

"Anything else you'd like to add?"

"Not at this time."

I leaned forward. "Sergeant Dunbar, what's the bottom line?"

He tilted his head and looked at me funny. "We're going to find the killer. We've got his DNA. He can't hide out forever. It'll look a lot better if he turns himself in now and claims responsibility."

I turned off the recording and set it on my lap. "I'm planning on talking to some people from Daphne's work today to see if they have any leads. Any of them in particular you recommend I start with?"

"I can't say anything at this time. But if you learn something interesting, let me know."

"Absolutely. I have the same goal you do, to catch whoever did this." I held his gaze.

With the creep leaving me threatening notes and a dead rose trapped in jail, I felt free to go all out, take risks, and, assuming he wasn't already behind bars, track down the killer.

CHAPTER SIXTEEN

Intermittent afternoon rainclouds parted, bathing the green one-story clapboard house before me in fresh sunlight. It sat on a large lot, in a forested area with plenty of foliage and space in between the neighbors.

One of the women I'd chatted with at Daphne's work had told me something particularly interesting, and I was here for a surprise visit with a familiar face.

A scraping sound emanated from the backyard. Abandoning my original path to the front door of his Jacksonville rental, I trudged past a skeletal pear tree toward the tall wooden fence bordering the side of the home. High grass tickled my ankles, making me itch, and left soaking watermarks on my gray canvas flats.

Pressing in closer to the fence, I called out his name. "Julien? Julien, is that you back there?"

The scraping sound stopped. "Hello?" he spoke in his thick French accent, metal equipment clanging. Wet leaves squished as he treaded in my direction.

The top half of his face appeared over the fence, looking down on me. I hadn't seen Julien since I'd stumbled over to his bar last week and he'd rejected me in his car.

"Hey," I picked at some dirt under my fingernail, trying to repress any feelings of humiliation. "It's Shelby. Remember me?" I joked.

"Hmmm," he scratched the top of his head. "I think you look familiar." His short cropped blond hair hung damply, with little droplets of water gleaming on his skin. The slightly disheveled, he-wasn't-even-trying look, only made him sexier. I could tell by the crinkles around his sea-green eyes, he was smiling.

"Do you always work outside in the rain?" I asked.

"You silly Southern California girls don't know a thing about rain." He shaded his forehead and looked toward the sky. "It has stopped for now. What happened to your face?"

I touched my bruised cheek. My makeup clearly wasn't hiding much. "Work injury. It's nothing."

"It looks bad."

"I'm fine," I said, willing my wounds to heal quickly so people would stop asking me what happened. In the meantime, maybe there was a better makeup tutorial video I could watch.

"How did you find me?" he asked.

"Your boss sold you out." I smirked. "I flattered him with stories of how I found some old footage of him winning Top Chef when the series first premiered. I gotta admit, winning on that cut-throat show; it's pretty impressive."

"That man would do anything so long as you stroke his ego."

I took a step back so I could see Julian a little clearer. His full face came into view. "Seems like everyone here in Ashland has a backstory," I said.

His lips pressed flat. The tone of our conversation turned more serious. "Why are you here, Shelby? Why'd you track me down?"

"Can I come inside?"

"We're being mysterious, aren't we?" His head disappeared behind the fence before the gate made a soft creaking sound as he pushed it open. He stood there, donning a clingy white T-shirt and a pair of faded jeans, looking me up and down for clues. "Come in."

"Thanks." I passed by close enough to catch his inviting caramelized coppery scent, like nothing I'd ever smelled on a man before. At thirty-six, he'd seen things I hadn't, and he had the appeal of an older man.

Taking in the large piece of property, I spotted a long wooden workbench sitting under an over-sized covered patio. Some sort of a clamp at the end of the bench held a raw branch of wood about the length and width of my arm. Tools rested within reaching distance on a blue tarp spread across uneven paver-stones. "What is that?" I asked, nodding to his setup.

"Oh," he put his hands on his hips. "It's a shaving horse. I'm working on a chair a client custom ordered. I'm carving the legs. Come, I'll show you how it works."

I followed his lead to the covered patio. "I didn't know you made furniture."

"Yeah, I can't tend bar forever. This is my dream. To open my own specialty furniture store. Look." He straddled the workbench and sat down.

Julien picked up a long saw with a wooden handle on each side. "This is a draw knife. I inherited it from my grandfather."

I pushed the sunglasses I was wearing to cover my bruises off my face and onto my head.

"When I work with this knife, I feel my grandfather's hands that made things before mine. It feels like he's guiding me." He rumbled in his thick French accent.

"You shipped this all the way over from France?"

"I can't work without it. I had to leave it behind when I was a UN peacekeeper in Africa, but when I got to the States, I had it shipped over."

"You're like Aiden on *Sex and The City.*"

"Yeah." His green eyes brightened. "My ex-wife used to tell me that. Emerson loved that show."

He turned back to his project. "Check it out. The shaving horse holds this new piece of wood I'm working on and the draw knife helps me change the shape of the wood into whatever I'm wanting to do with it."

I watched him drag the drawknife over the branch, scraping off the bark. His sturdy hands gripped the tool, pulling, reaching, confident, and fast. I pushed away the thoughts of what he'd done to me with those hands the times we were alone together, and instead, I tried to imagine the more sinister things he might have committed with his hands under the cloak of darkness.

I'd come to his home on a mission. "Speaking of your ex," I kicked at a loose paver-stone, "I've been covering the story of the murders on Belle Street."

"Yeah." He gripped the drawknife tighter and scraped deeper.

"Yes, and I was talking to one of Daphne DeLuca's former coworkers at the Shakespeare Festival office about anyone she thought might be involved in Daphne's murder.

The woman mentioned Daphne had recently dumped several of the guys she was dating for a mystery man. The coworker was pretty sure he was a Frenchman."

Julien stopped working, his face blank, not giving away any clues of his thoughts. "Yes?"

"Obviously, I thought about you. You move in similar social circles. Both very attractive and available. You were troubled the last time I saw you, that night I visited you at the bar. You said it'd been a rough week."

His jaw tensed. "You don't think I killed Daphne, do you?"

"Were you two dating?" I asked.

"You're not here for personal reasons, are you?"

Biting the inside of my cheek, I said, "I'm not trying to run an exposé on your love life Julien, we're friends. I respect your privacy. But I'm investigating Daphne's murder. It's my job. And the last woman I spoke to unknowingly led me to you."

His shoulders slumped, and his spine bowed, as if all of his inner fortitude was unraveling. "We weren't dating. It was more than that."

My pulse beat faster. "What were you?"

"Daphne and I were engaged."

"You were—what? Wow." I stepped back in surprise. My eyes traveled toward his hands again. I noticed the thick silver band on his left index finger, and my heart broke a little.

Had he been seeing Daphne the times he was with me? I knew it shouldn't matter. I wasn't looking for a commitment. But I didn't want to feel completely unimportant either, like I was nothing more than another girl to get him through the night.

"Did she give that to you?" I asked, fearful of his answer.

He nodded, his lips trembling with sadness. "It all happened so fast. I met her only about two and a half months ago. Within a week we knew we were meant to be."

A feeling of relief eased my heart as I did the math. He'd met Daphne after we'd stopped seeing each other.

"I loved her more than I've ever loved anything or anyone," he continued. "I wanted to shout out our love to the world, I still do, but she said 'no'." His words spilled forth like he was in confession.

"Daphne said to keep us a secret until after my divorce was complete. She was so thoughtful, she didn't want Emerson to be upset that I'd found another woman before we were divorced."

I fiddled with the sunglasses on my head. As much as I liked Daphne, she didn't seem like the kind of girl who would end up marrying a blue-collar man. Even if her mom said Daphne didn't care about money, a bartender with dreams of opening a furniture shop wasn't going to give her a comfortable lifestyle. Not like the other men in her life could've provided.

"How discreet were you with Daphne? Did you go out on dates in town?"

"We spent all of our time here, well, a couple times at her place, but late at night, after everyone else was in bed."

He must've been the guy Daphne's roommates complained about her bringing home after hours. It was possible she was only using Julien for his body before she settled on a more prosperous husband-to-be. Had she tried to break it off after she grew tired of him?

Despite how well I thought I knew him, maybe his pride

was destroyed and that sent him over the edge. It didn't seem possible, but I wondered if my sweet Julien's humiliation could have turned him to violence.

"Julien," I hesitated, feeling uncomfortable asking him my next question. "Did you give the police your blood sample? They've been testing all the men Daphne knew, you know, to rule them out as suspects."

His head hung low. "Daphne wanted to wait for the divorce to go through. She was excited to make the announcement. I'm still respecting her wishes."

That didn't look good.

Then another thought occurred to me, one that in my mind, made a whole lot more sense. A man like Julien could make a woman crazy with jealousy. What if the killer was a woman? Someone who knew Julien and resented his relationship with Daphne? What if his ex-wife knew about his secret relationship?

This was the scenario I wanted to believe in.

"You must have been so happy to have met Daphne," I said, trying to ease into a new line of questions. "I remember how depressed you were over the separation from your wife."

He swiped away a rogue tear. "I thought Emerson was the love of my life. If it weren't for Daphne, I don't know if I would've recovered. She made all my heartache make sense. I like to think I married Emerson so she could lead me here to Ashland where I would meet Daphne."

If Emerson had any clue how Julien felt, it had to have hurt. I tried to picture Emerson in my head. Was she a strong woman? Strong enough to murder two women at once?

Julien tilted his head with suspicion. "Please don't be using this in a story, Shelby. I can't bear to be seen as Daphne's secret lover on the news. The man who might have done her in."

My skin prickled with nervous heat. I didn't believe he was guilty. He was a sensitive man, he'd never hurt anybody. "This isn't about revealing you as a potential suspect. But you do need to go to the police and give them your DNA, Julien. Come clean and clear your name before they figure it out themselves. They won't announce you to the press or anything. You'll still be able to keep upholding Daphne's wishes."

He hung his head in surrender. "It'll be a relief to tell the authorities. I worked for the French police, remember? I know what it looks like that I didn't come forward straightaway."

"I've built a relationship with the lead detective. I'll give him a heads-up and let him know you're going to come in tomorrow, okay? Is it a deal?"

"Sure."

A passing cloud shrouded the sunshine once again. "Why did you and Emerson break up? You never told me the story."

He grimaced. "It's quite embarrassing really. Emerson had a great love for white wine and other men. I walked in on her once. That's an image you don't forget. I stayed a few more months after that. But every time I touched her, I pictured her with that other man. It was too much."

"Was she always so wild and rebellious?"

He swatted away a small brown moth, its wings beating to escape. "That's a good way to describe it. I think she joined Greenpeace for a fresh start. She was a civil engineer before we met, and one day she quit her good job, gave away all her things, and tried to start a new life."

"That's awfully drastic."

Julien began scaping at the wood again. "It didn't work. When we moved to the states, she began drinking more, flirting and sneaking around. She slipped into her old ways."

"And then you two were on-again, off-again for at least a year. I remember you told me Emerson wanted to get back together, but you were afraid she would hurt you again."

"Reconciliation wasn't a good idea. But I was tempted. I loved her still and I hated being alone."

"Daphne saved you from Emerson."

Julien gazed off beyond the property line as dark clouds stacked in the sky. His expression looked lost in time. "Daphne was everything. I would miss her before she even left the room."

Agitated, he jammed the drawknife into the wood, pushing and pulling so hard it splintered and snapped. "When they discover the man who did this to her, I will scorch every inch of the landscape he called his life." He tossed the drawknife to the ground and wiped the sweat from his brow with his forearm.

I asked Julian outright, ignoring yet another incoming text message from my mom. "Do you think Emerson somehow found out about Daphne?"

"No. I'm not as simple-minded as you think. I see where you're going with this, Shelby. But it's not like that. Emerson had no idea. I refused to see her, or any other woman after I met Daphne. Emerson was busy traveling to Portland looking for a new job up there. She was preparing for another move. She must've found something because she packed up a moving truck about three weeks ago and left town. *Before* what happened to Daphne. Not after."

"I'm so sorry for your loss, Julien," I said, not convinced

of Emerson's innocence one bit. She could have plotted the murder, moved to Portland as an alibi, and then driven back Halloween night to kill her ex's lover. Julien was a former cop. Somewhere deep down he had to realize it was a possibility.

Rubbing his ring and twisting it between his fingers, Julien said, "I still believe, you know? Even now."

"Believe what?"

"That Daphne and I were destined to be together. We were both meant to feel true love. She will never experience pain again. And for that I am grateful, but now I'm the one who has to suffer. I wish I could get her off my mind." Tears flooded his eyes as weighted clouds broke open, releasing the soft patter of raindrops pinging the tin patio roof. A distant roll of thunder clapped in the distance, and a bolt of blue lightning zapped the darkening sky.

"Sounds like a storm's blowing in," I said, not sure what to do or say next.

He looked up at me with wounded eyes. "I'm sorry for how things ended when I took you home the other day."

I bit my lip, feeling a new sort of tension build between us. "I get it. No hard feelings."

He swung his leg around his work bench and stood up, stepping a little closer, his coppery scent provoking fond memories. "I was in pain. Am in pain," he said. "I needed time to believe it was all real. It's still hard to accept she's gone."

"I'm sure," I said.

"Men are not good on their own." He stood with his legs slightly parted.

I remembered those washboard abs hiding underneath

his white T-shirt. That black and yellow tiger tattooed across his heart. His flashes of heat followed by hungry desperation.

Julien moved in closer and the intense desire to touch him nearly overwhelmed me. If I let him, he'd kiss me. I could feel it.

Thoughts of Jack filtered through my consciousness, of how much he cared for me, of how much I was falling for him. Julien was my easiest opportunity to end it before Jack sucked me in completely. I needed to protect us both. Not to mention I was frustrated after the way he shut me down last night. Julien looked better than my favorite ice cream.

He gazed at me, making firm eye contact.

Wasn't this exactly what I wanted, a beautiful man, no strings attached? No taking it slow, no over-protection. Guys didn't get much hotter than Julien, and with him grieving for Daphne, I was in zero danger of getting caught up in a commitment.

Julian reached out and gently grazed my fingers with his. "We were good together, no?"

His presence was intoxicating.

CHAPTER SEVENTEEN

When things got bad, I made them worse. Hooking up with Julien felt like another one of the reckless choices I made to escape the world around me.

Revving on the engine, I blasted the heater of my Escalade and waved goodbye as Julien stood with his hands in his jean pockets to see me off. The rainstorm had passed, but Oregon's steel-gray, impenetrable sky hung heavy, promising more turbulent weather on the horizon. I was already regretting sleeping with Julien.

Mud and debris kicked up as I sped down the slippery dirt road leading away from his home. Shutting out any new thoughts of my personal problems, I planned to do a little more research on Julien's estranged wife.

I wasn't convinced the murderer on Belle Street had to be a man. The third roommate living in the house, the only witness, was scared and hiding from the killer, plus it was dark, she could've gotten it wrong.

Shortly after I turned the corner and Julien was out of sight, my phone rang.

"Where are you?" Jack's voice rang over my Bluetooth

when I answered the phone.

"Jacksonville." I hit the gas pedal. "I had a lead I wanted to talk to."

"You told me you would go home after talking to Sergeant Dunbar."

As usual, he was tracking my moves, depriving me of even an inch of personal room. "I ended up with some new ideas I wanted to follow up on."

Jack let out an exasperated sigh. "Am I coming over to you tonight or are you sleeping at my place again?"

"Dunbar said those losers are locked up for at least another two weeks. We're not in any immediate danger."

Flashes of green foliage outside my windows gradually took the shape of pine trees as I slowed for the stop sign up ahead.

"So what are you saying?" Jack asked.

"I'm saying, I'm gonna sleep alone at my place tonight." After what I'd done, I needed to put some space between us, give whatever it was we were building toward time to cool down. I tried to rationalize my behavior, telling myself that even if I hadn't just been with another man, there was no sense in hanging out with Jack so often. I'd made a mistake letting him in too close, especially considering I planned on leaving Ashland in my past as soon as this case wrapped up.

Jack, of course, didn't give up. "Why don't you wait to stay on your own until after we get your taser? That way if anything comes up, you've got a weapon. Hanging out'll be fun, plus I'll grab dinner."

I slapped on my blinker to turn left onto the main road. "Sergeant Dunbar didn't even take those notes seriously."

"What's he supposed to say? Women get stalked all the time and the police can't do a thing about it. Then one day, you hear the poor woman's been shot to death, or set on fire, or who knows what else."

"Morbid much?" I pulled down my sun visor, to ward off the glare from the clouds, and shut off the heat.

"I bet if you were Sergeant Dunbar's daughter, he'd find those notes threatening."

"You're being a little dramatic."

"Whatever."

"I'll text you my address. We can have dinner. Then you'll go home."

———

By the time I'd showered, changed into sweatpants, and stalked Julien's ex on social media—a natural blonde beauty with a commanding presence—Jack knocked on my front door, white take-out boxes in hand.

"What'd you get?" I hugged my arms around my waist, trying to stave off the chill blowing inside.

White puffs of carbon dioxide floated into the night air as Jack shuffled the mud off his shoes. "Hi to you, too."

With his almond-shaped eyes and relaxed sensual expression, Jack radiated hope and kindness. I remembered how it felt when he kissed me last night, how different it was to spend time with someone who truly cared for me.

"Come on in," I said halfheartedly, motioning toward the stairwell that led up to the main floor. It was nice of him to bring dinner, it would have been even nicer if he'd given me some space.

Once upstairs, he followed me across polished maple floors into my state-of-the-art kitchen.

"You finally let me see your place."

"What do you think?" I asked.

"Fancy Schmancy." Jack chuckled, setting down our food on the white marble countertop. "So you're right, you do have a nicer pad than the rest of us. Who owns the big house up front?"

"The Moreno Family, they're from San Francisco. They built this apartment for one of their moms to live in during the summer months. After she passed away, they decided to rent it out below market price to the right tenant. I guess they trust me. They're hardly ever around. I have the entire backyard to myself most days."

Jack peered out the window overlooking the lush, immaculately landscaped backyard. "It's huge. I bet that hot tub feels amazing."

"Yeah," I said, still feeling a little embarrassed about how luxurious my home was compared to his. "It just feels big because of the open floorplan. It's really kind of small when you count in the bedrooms."

"You live alone and have more than one bedroom?" he asked with a hint of disbelief in his voice.

"It's for when either of my parents visit."

His posture softened. "How's your dad?"

My arms brushed against his as I began opening the takeout boxes, inhaling the steam as it rose off the sweet and sour chicken, brown rice, and beef and broccoli. "The surgery was this afternoon as planned. It went well. My mom sent me a text saying he's home recuperating. I would have flown out there, but with this giant bruise on my face and all the other cuts and scrapes, I didn't want to freak them out. Besides, they don't know I have a week off from the station." I shrugged. "Dad didn't want me taking time away from covering my story."

Jack began to search the cabinets, pulling out plates and drinking glasses. "That's why you worked today, isn't it? Distraction. Also explains why you're acting kind of funny."

"Yeah." I walked toward the sink, realizing Jack was at least half right. I hadn't thought about Dad's surgery more than a handful of times today. It was too hard.

After I talked with Jack over breakfast this morning, I'd made a quick call to wish Dad luck, responded to Mom's message when she updated me after the surgery that he was okay, and otherwise completely blocked the surgery out of my consciousness, like his cancer didn't exist. No wonder I'd been so reckless with Julien. It wasn't just some crazy attraction, or complete self-sabotage of a potentially awesome relationship with Jack. I was blocking out any worry about my dad.

"Chopsticks or forks?" I asked. "The silverware's in here." I pointed to the correct drawer.

"Chopsticks," he said, pulling them out of the plastic take-out bag. "I'm glad your dad's doing well."

Ignoring his comment, I stepped over to the fridge. "Beer or water?"

"Do you even have to ask?"

It was a silly question. I grabbed each of us a Stella Artois.

Jack leaned his back against the countertop and looked at me. "How are you?"

I could feel the blush of shame climb the sides of my

neck. He was asking about my well-being because of my dad, but I couldn't help visualizing the details of what else happened this afternoon. "I'm good. Let's eat on the couch."

We set up our plates on the large round blond-wood coffee table my mother had bought for me. Then we sat down on the comfy suede couch. I'd tried to talk my mom out of buying me furniture, but you can't really say no when it's shipped directly to your house. That was my mom for you, she had the subtlety of a combustion engine. I flicked on the television to some cool lo-fi trip-hop for background music.

"So who was the lead on your story? Anyone we've talked to before?" Jack asked.

My heart bled with guilt. "Different people Daphne knew. I was thinking again it might be a woman who committed the crimes. One of Daphne's lover's ex's might've been involved."

"What makes you think that?"

"Just a hunch."

"Yeah?" he tilted his head with curiosity.

"This one ex, Emerson Bisset, was having trouble letting go of her husband. They were separated, but he was always letting her back in. Then he met Daphne and he was finished with her, wanted the divorce finalized, refused to see her. That could make a woman go crazy."

"Depends on who the husband is, I guess. Did you talk to this lover guy?"

My mouth went dry and I no longer felt like eating. "Yeah."

"Today?"

I nodded.

"And, of course, you went alone. Why didn't you call me, Shelbs? I would have waited in the car if you were worried about me stepping on your toes."

Was he always so suffocating? "One of Daphne's coworkers clued me in and I tracked him down. I don't need a chaperone everywhere I go."

He tapped his chopsticks against the sweet and sour chicken, his lips sealed in a frustrated frown.

"I understand why you're so over-protective, but it's not healthy."

"You're so extra jumpy tonight." He laughed as if he was joking, but we both knew he wasn't.

I narrowed my eyes at him, my defenses growing, "You don't own me, you know."

"Shelby, you're reading this all wrong." He stabbed his chopstick into a piece of chicken. "So," he said, as if he was going to change the subject. "What kind of dude was Daphne dating? Was he an older guy or someone our age?"

"Older. Maybe thirty-six, I think. He's a bartender in Ashland and he wants to open his own furniture store."

"Huh," Jack said without further comment.

Rain began to pelt the windowsills, a new storm unleashing. "I texted Sergeant Dunbar to look into this guy's ex. Dunbar didn't seem too convinced, though, that a woman has that kind of strength. But, why not? Women commit crimes of passion all the time."

"Yeah." Jack eyed the chicken skewered to his chopstick. Our food was getting cold. "But besides the fact that a woman could be capable of killing Daphne and Melissa, why do you think this particular woman might've done it?"

"I told you, jealousy. Oh yeah, and Julien, her ex, told

me she just moved back to Portland. It's suspicious."

Jack took a bite of food and a sip of his beer. "Why don't you suspect the guy did it, since he was Daphne's actual lover? Seems like the more obvious suspect."

"Because Julien's a nice guy."

The rain picked up and slapped against the window-panes, casting the outside world into a blur. "Gotcha."

"You're acting weird." I looked over at him before focusing back on my plate.

"I'm acting weird?" Jack stuffed a piece of chicken into his mouth "You're the one who's totally off. What is it, did you sleep with him or something?" He laughed again, but this time there was a dagger behind his words.

I was tired of his accusations. "Honestly?" Defense and guilt rose in my stomach. "I did."

"What?" Jack's body went stiff as he looked at me with wide injured eyes. "When?"

"This afternoon." The words came out in a bruising whisper. I could already feel my heart breaking.

I jumped off the couch and paced the length of the living room. My adrenaline raced. "How many times have I told you the most important thing to me right now is my career and my family? It's not like I ever led you on."

"So, what was last night? And everything we shared this morning?" He placed his hands on his knees, sitting forward in a daze. "What am I to you, Shelby?"

"You're the one who didn't want to get together with me last night, remember? We're just two friends hanging out."

"You sure have a funny way of showing it," he spat, the edge of his anger sharpening. "You're the worst friend I've ever had, Shelby."

Why did sleep I with Julien? Why did I tell Jack? Why couldn't I behave like a normal human being who didn't destroy everything good in her life?

The lo-fi song switched from soft and romantic to something more frantic. Jack's eyes focused on me, lasering in with a fury. "I sacrificed so that we could have something more meaningful than just a hookup."

"Gold star, Jack. Everything you do is right, and everything I do is messed up and wrong." My defensive posture turned to vengeance. "You know what your problem is?"

"My problem?" His jaw pulsed. "Sure, Shelby, why don't you tell me?"

"I'm too much of a challenge for you and you can't stand it."

His mouth fell open.

"You said so yourself, you're used to getting any woman you want. You never had to try." I pushed up the sleeves on my sweatshirt and placed my hands on my hips. "Why don't you go call Kaya again and hook up with her? She's easy, isn't she?"

"Kaya's a good girl. She doesn't deserve to be anyone's second choice." He tightened the shoelaces on his Vans and stood up. "But, hey, as far as you and I go, maybe it's for the best. That guy Julien's an easier score for you, fewer strings attached."

He strode toward the stairs leading down to the front door.

"Where are you going?" I could feel something inside me collapsing. Perhaps it was my common sense finally kicking in, telling me how badly I'd messed up.

My heart hurt, already feeling the loss of him. I didn't

know what I wanted and I hated it. I wanted Jack, but not too much, I wanted everything about him, but nothing at all. More than anything, I wanted to know what I wanted. "I thought you were supposed to be protecting me."

"You don't need protecting, you said it yourself." He took the stairs at a racer's speed.

"But it's raining outside," I argued.

Jack waved up his hand in a sharp goodbye before slamming the door shut behind him. My head pulsed with a sickening realization.

I'd ruined us.

———

About twenty minutes later the doorbell rang and I rushed the stairs, full of hope. Maybe he'd changed his mind. We could talk it out. I could apologize for getting out of control. Maybe he was willing to fight for me.

I yanked open the door to the dead of night. A taped piece of folded computer paper lifted in the wet wind and then settled back flat, damp with rain.

> I'm still here.
> This, Ms. Day, is your final warning.
> Do you want to live for another morning?

CHAPTER EIGHTEEN

It felt like the note was going to erupt in my trembling hands. My legs went numb. My heartbeat threatened to explode out of my chest.

Wild with anxiety, I slammed the front door and locked it shut. The dreadlocked man was in jail, it couldn't be him. That also meant, it could be anybody. Maybe a coworker trying to scare me out of my position?

No, this was too threatening. None of my colleagues would push me this way. The news business was cutthroat, but not even Lily would do something so violent.

The note wrinkled in my fist, dampening in a cold sweat. *Where was Jack?* He'd said he would come back.

Could he be the one? Could he be angry enough to do this to scare me? This note appeared right after he stormed out. Impossible. I could never believe he would do something so vile to torture me.

Memories of the crime scene photos flashed in my mind. What if I was the next target? Chills shot down my spine. My body ached as I mentally combed my apartment thinking of things I could use as weapons, where I could sneak out a window, where I'd left my cell phone.

Shoving the note into my back pocket, I charged up the stairs and ran as fast as I could, past the glass windows, into the kitchen. My phone rested on the counter, screen down. Heart pounding in my chest and salty tears slipping down my cheeks, I snatched my phone and the long purple chef's knife from the drawer.

My brain raced with every sort of possibility. Where was this person? Were they still outside? Who was it?

No one on my suspect list had been cleared by the police: Melissa's boyfriend, the third roommate who escaped injury, Julien or his estranged wife. Or maybe it was someone we hadn't discovered yet, someone lurking in the shadows or walking beside me in plain sight?

I leaned against the blank wall of my living room and sank to my knees. Heavy tears slipped down my cheeks and wet my lips. I shivered at the thought of what those girls went through.

Ten, perhaps twenty seconds passed before I sprinted into my bedroom, slamming and locking the door behind me. I shrugged off the idea of calling 911, it was pointless. There was no illegal incident to report, no person to arrest.

It was just a note. Sergeant Dunbar had already told me, at best they would keep the information on file in case something bigger occurred. The police couldn't help me.

I dropped the knife and punched the pillow on my bed with fists clamped so tight my fingernails cut into my palms. Sweat poured down my back. My teeth gnashed with self-hatred.

My dad had cancer and I wasn't even there to drive with him to his surgery. I'd ruined my relationship with Jack. I hadn't made a single dent in coming closer to catching the killer.

I was hurting every single person that mattered to me, and no matter what I did now, I'd only make it worse. Why was I even here? If I stayed in Ashland and pursued this story, I could end up dead. It was stupid to think that, after years of self-sabotage, I was anything more than a spoiled rich girl from Los Angeles using her dad's money to pretend to build some sort of meaningful life.

Investigative Reporter. Who was I kidding? I was a joke.

I paced across my dimly lit bedroom, repeatedly checking the closet, window, and door. I had to go. I had to leave. I'd take what mattered most and drive straight home tonight. Mom could hire movers to get the rest.

The rain continued its assault. I peered through the window, shuddering at the thought of who might be outside watching. Plump drops raced ahead of gravity, trailing watery streaks across plateglass. My clouded reflection looked back at me as faint as a ghost.

I needed to act—fast.

On trembling legs, I stopped pacing and plodded toward the sleek modern desk, pulling open the large bottom drawer where I stashed a duffle bag filled with emergency clothes, $300 cash, and a spare pack of cigarettes. I pulled one out and opened the window. Just this once, I'd break the rules. Running the lighter along the tip until the tobacco curled in the flame, I inhaled the arid leaves, the smoke powdering my lungs and failing to calm the tremors in my hand.

Tilting my chin upward, I loosened my lips and exhaled, wisps of smoke curling into the damp air. Common sense seeped back in. Running away wasn't a good option. It wouldn't fix what I'd done to Jack and me. It wouldn't make my father happy. My mother would simply move on to something new to obsess over.

Running away would only do one thing; satisfy the stalker. Perhaps he or she would let it go. But where would that leave me? I'd probably settle into a production job that Cousin Inna could get for me. I'd stay in the newsroom, but without the necessary on-air experience, I'd probably never work on camera again. My and my father's dream would be dead.

I'd lose interest in work, meet some guy, and get swept away in the excitement of a temporary distraction. I'd end up like the girls I went to high school with; married and miserable, spending my afternoons gossiping on Facebook Pyramid Scheme groups while ignoring my kids, only to drag myself to the therapist because I was so depressed. My failure would cling like a relentless shadow loitering beside me, reminding me I'd thrown away my chance at something special.

In the quiet darkness, my cigarette's blue-white smoke circled around my neck, choking me. The blurry outline of a murderer wielding a gleaming knife, flashed in my mind. He used fear like a smoke bomb to gas me out of my home so he could track my moves.

I realized if I fled Ashland now, I could lead the killer straight to my family. He was smart, he knew how to get to me without involving the cops. LAPD wouldn't do a thing about a supposedly nonthreatening stalker until it was far too late.

Pacing back and forth in quick short bursts, I clamored

to devise a plan. Pictures of college friends and journalism heroes framed in washi-tape on pale-yellow walls, smiled back at me, reminding me of all I'd already accomplished and the reasons why I came here. Once I'd set my mind on transforming myself into a better person, I never doubted it was possible. Thinking back, I couldn't remember a single time I'd ever given in and readjusted my desires to suit failure.

My heart hammered in my chest as my right hand clenched back into a fist. The violent energy that raged inside me like a hurricane whenever I felt trapped—exploded.

I wasn't going to give up investigating the murders I'd promised to pursue. I wasn't going to run home and hide. This jerk-off leaving me threatening notes and a dead flower wasn't going play nice. But I had a newsflash for him, I was meaner. *When someone hits hard, Shelby Day punches back harder.*

The doorbell rang. My stomach lurched. Deep penetrating terror laced with fury. I grabbed the kitchen knife and tucked it in the elastic band of my leggings. Whatever faced me on the other side, I would stand my ground.

CHAPTER NINETEEN

The December morning stung my lips and fingers. I'd parked the news car forty miles northwest from the station, off a snow-covered dirt road in a remote area of Grants Pass. The icy path between two large oak trees led to a shaded, secluded home. My plan: knock on the front door and speak a few words with the occupant. At the very least.

It had been Jack who'd knocked on my door after the last note was delivered. I'd kept it shoved in my pocket and said nothing as he walked without a word to the guest bedroom. He barely looked at me and refused to talk to me. That was an endless three weeks ago, and the time following had slogged by without a single threatening note or any new leads on the case. Equally challenging, Jack refused to speak to me. I couldn't blame him.

More than a full month had passed since the murders. December arrived, and I worried that the murder investigation was going to turn into a cold case. Surely things would grow quieter for the people of Ashland as the distractions of the Christmas season swung into full force. I couldn't help thinking, though, that this would be the first Christmas without Melissa and Daphne. The murder may be brushed aside by Ashland, but it surely wouldn't be forgotten by the families. And it certainly wouldn't be overlooked by me.

Thankfully, Alex Haskell appreciated the way I'd covered his story before he and Melissa's third roommate were exonerated as suspects by police. Alex had messaged me over Instagram this morning with news of a rumor circulating town. A man told several friends he'd overheard an angry restaurateur swear up a storm about a bad rating Melissa issued to his fish and chips joint a few days before her murder. The speculation went against the prevailing theory that Daphne was the killer's intended target, and despite all my worries about confronting the potential killer on my own, it piqued my interest. I felt like I had nothing to lose, so I packed my gear and my taser, and went for it.

Gripping my equipment for security on that quiet Sunday morning, I rang the doorbell. A heavyset man sporting a red face and a mop of messy brown curls flung open the front door. "Hello?"

"Hi." I took an involuntary step backward and sized him up. Compared to me, he was a big man, but to everybody else he was probably a normal graying guy with an old restaurant T-shirt covering his beer belly. Tiny broken blood vessels covered his bulbous nose and puffy cheeks. "Russell King?"

"Who wants to know?" He stared at me intently, either because he knew exactly who I was, or because he had no idea who I was and he wondered what I was doing there.

My chest tightened with fear. I had hoped I could tell instantly if he recognized me or not. The look on his face gave me no clues as to if I were safe or not. But I refused to give up. "I'm Shelby Day with *NBC 4 News*."

"What do you want?" he grunted.

"Sorry to show up unannounced." I filled in the blank silence with a slight tremble in my voice. "Your number listed online wasn't working. But it gave me this address. Have you heard about the murders that happened on Belle Street in Ashland? One of the girls who was killed on Halloween, Melissa Rossi, she gave your restaurant a C rating. Do you remember?"

"What do you mean 'remember?' What are you saying?"

"People are talking, implying that you were pretty angry with Melissa. I thought maybe you'd want to say something on camera to get your story out. You know, clear your name, let people know the truth."

He scratched his head and twisted his lips in thought. I held my breath, both hoping and not hoping he would say 'yes' to my offer.

He looked me up and down with a glimmer of delight in his upturned lips. "Sure," he answered, as if the ugly rumors and a reporter showing up on his doorstep were a little more thrilling than he was willing to let on. "But only if you promise to come back and do a story on my restaurant in the summer."

To his left, an old, greyhound lay on its side on the tiled entry. The Weimaraner raised its head an inch or so off the floor and glanced at me through milky-white cataracted eyes. I reached out to pet it, but it didn't even notice my hand. The poor thing looked exhausted by life.

Beyond the dog, I could see straight through the dusty house, past the half-opened dirty slider door, right into the backyard. I heard the rush of the Rogue River beyond the yellow grass patched with melting snow.

I clutched my tripod tighter in my left hand. "It's kind of a cold day to leave the doors open." I shuffled my booted feet to keep warm, stalling for time to think.

"Cold?" He glanced over his shoulder before looking back in my direction. I could feel his eyes run the length of me. "Sure you're cold, you're so tiny you don't have any natural insulation."

A nervous shiver in my bones made me wish I'd asked Jack to join me. Even though he wasn't talking to me, I was certain he still would've come. Kaya probably would've been able to dig up another reporter to send out with me, if I'd asked her. I would've even put up with a forty-five-minute drive enduring the "Lily" show if it meant she'd have come with me. My right hand patted my back pocket, reassuring me my phone was close. The taser rested inside my camera bag.

People knew where I was. This man, whoever he was or what he'd done, wouldn't take the risk of hurting me when he would so easily get caught.

"Fine, come on in." He waved, poker faced.

Faded family photos, blanketed in thin layers of dust, adorned the stained-wood side table next to a worn green couch in the living room.

"Is your wife home?" I asked knowing full well how unlikely it was any modern woman decorated her home like it was the 1970's. His place was straight out of the *Brady Bunch*, all shades of orange and puke green.

"The only lady that would stick with me is *The Hungry Fisherman*. I'm married to my restaurant." He grinned.

"I get that." I nodded, feeling slightly more relaxed about

our arrangement. I could relate to making your career your life. "Wow, you really have a gorgeous view from the deck. I bet you sit out there all the time."

"Sure do, with a coffee in the mornin' and a Heineken at night. We could do an interview out there if you want."

"Oh, great! That sounds perfect. A Heineken and a nice pack of cigarettes, don't you think?" I stepped around the dog and into the shag-carpeted living room.

"Nope, I don't smoke. Gotta live long enough to pay off the restaurant, ya know?"

The man slid his hand through his bushy hair. I watched his brow wrinkle in thought as sweat glistened and slowly made its way down the side of his face. He wiped the back of his hand across his forehead, odd considering how cold it was. "This place is mine now. Both my parents passed a couple years back."

"Oh, my gosh, I'm so sorry to hear that."

I thought of my own dad, the most important man in my life.

Russell shrugged, "It's been a while, I don't cry over it anymore. Mom was real sick. A lot of misery on her end. More on my dad's, probably, he loved her too much to see her like that."

"I can imagine." I tiptoed around the mess of culinary magazines and old newspapers, trying to put more space in between us.

He stared at me. "You're not the first reporter to come out here."

"Oh, I'm not? Somebody else came to talk to you about the murders on Belle Street?"

"No."

"What did the other reporter come out here for?" I laughed, "A good review for your 'wife' or something?"

He squinted his eyes. Another thick trail of sweat rolled from his forehead, down his cheek, and fell to his second chin. My muscles tensed up again. This man was holding the cards and flaunting it, hiding pieces of information.

I bit the inside of my lip and checked the stoic dog from the corner of my eye for signs of life.

"I wish. My dad couldn't see my mom suffer any longer. Murder-suicide."

I felt my eyes widen. "I'm so sorry, that's horrible."

"Ah, shut it. Really, it was a mercy killing. No use crying over it, won't change the past."

"You must have been devastated."

"It was for the best. Mom's in peace. Dad gets to be with her, nagging and all." He laughed, a swollen drinker's chuckle. "He'll never get rid of her. Poor bastard." The man cleared his throat. "Everybody wins, parents are happy, dog stays fed, and I can bring women here instead of back to my old apartment."

Feeling eager to get our interview going, I shifted my weight. "The camera gear's getting kinda heavy. Can I set up outside?" I took a step toward the kitchen that rested between the living room and the back slider, hoping to keep moving forward through the house. If I stayed in motion, it'd be harder for him to rope me into conversation.

"I can show you around the rest of the house first," he offered.

I envisioned decomposing bodies stacked waist deep, stuffed inside a secret bedroom closet. Russell King may not have been the killer, or my stalker, but he was definitely creepy. Better to stay outdoors for a quicker escape. "I'm actually only allowed an hour and a half for a news story, it took me forty minutes to get here, so I really don't have time to stay for every long," I lied. "They're waiting for me back at the station to get on to the next story. You wouldn't believe how carefully they monitor every little thing we do."

"If you say so," he said, grabbing a jacket from a pile of old clothes on the couch. "You know, you're right. It is a little cold now. Let's do this in the living room." He stepped in front of me, cutting off my forward movement to the porch.

The hairs on my arms lifted. "Sure." I set down my camera bag beside me. Facing him while I kneeled down, I opened the legs on my tripod and prepared to grab a lavalier mic for him to string up his grungy Fish Jacket. "Let's go ahead and get this on you while I set up the camera. I just have a few quick questions." I approached him.

"What're you gonna ask me?" he said as I handed him the tiny attachable microphone.

"Nothing too bad. I'm going to tell you I heard Melissa Rossi gave you a C rating, and then ask 'how do you feel about that, Mr. King? People are starting to say it was a low blow.' You can say that you're married to your restaurant, you care about it a lot, this is your chance to set them straight."

His grin quickly changed to a hurt expression. "She was wrong to do that. *The Hungry Fisherman* was having an off day. I asked her to re-evaluate it and she refused."

He seemed agitated, I backed up, moving myself closer to the front door, trying to avoid eye contact. I got the feeling he was about to spout antics about his restaurant. At least I'd told him I only had a few minutes, if worse came to worst, I could cut him off and leave early. "It would be good to talk about how great your food is too. This way you could get people to come to your restaurant." I said, hoping that discussing something other than how hurt he was by Melissa's rating would put him in a better mood.

He scratched at the palm of his hand furiously. "Why do women have to be so hard to get along with?"

"It probably wasn't personal, she probably had a manager following her pretty closely or something." I tried to deflect his boiling anger. My skin warmed with panic, my internal red flag waving with alarm. "Can you put the mic on while I set up the camera?"

He smiled with a poisonous mock benevolence and spoke slowly, in a dramatized high-pitched voice, as if he were mimicking a young girl speaking. "I'm sorry, Mr. King, but I can't do that. We have to follow protocol."

I could feel my eyes grow wide. What was he talking about?

"What was that?" I asked with shaking hands, trying to avert eye contact while reaching for my bag. He was probably just weird, but it wouldn't hurt to keep my taser extra close just in case.

His eyes bulged like a madman. "That's what Melissa Rossi told me when I asked for a re-evaluation. To give me a second chance. But no, she couldn't bend any rules. She had 'to follow protocol,' whatever that meant."

Pin pricks of sweat formed around the base of my neck.

He drew in slow steady breaths and my eyes involuntarily followed his hand. For the first time, I noticed he had his right hand in his sweatpants.

He mimicked Melissa Rossi's voice once again, "I'm sure

everything will turn out fine. You don't need to worry."

My mouth went dry, instinct took the wheel. I dove down to unzip my camera bag for protection. Just as my hand finished dragging the pull-tag across the length of the zipper—he lunged and connected.

"This is what I should have done to her," he whispered furtively as he made contact. His hands reached for my shoulders pushing me backwards. "You girls think you have all the power."

I felt myself falling. The back of my head whacked against the shag-carpeted floor. A low guttural moan punctured my ears.

Struggling, I opened my eyes for help. The dog lay motionless, as helpless as me, and I realized those agonizing moans were mine.

I could smell fish on his thick calloused hand when he pressed it against my mouth to silence me. With his knees pinning my hips, he used his free hand to yank down the elastic waistline on his sweatpants. My mind spun as I struggled for air. From the corner of my eye, I could see the nearly opened camera bag, almost within reach.

Wrenching my head back and forth, I loosened the seal of his fleshy hand forced against my mouth. While distracted with his sweatpants, he lifted his palm just enough. I saw my chance. I jerked my head back and bit hard into the side of his palm.

Now it was his turn to scream. He rocked backward, shaking his hand, and moved just enough to loosen his grip on my body. I slid myself from under his legs, clawing at the carpet, and dragged myself toward the camera bag. He stumbled, reaching forward to grab at me, but I was faster.

"You're finished." He cocked his arm and formed a fist. *Too late, asshole.* "Who has the power now?" I kicked him in the face.

He reeled and sputtered, buying me the time to seize the taser from my bag and hoist it forward. I aimed the pins toward his bulging torso. His T-shirt was lifted, exposing vulnerable white flesh.

I held onto the trigger, my finger gripped tightly in terror. Two prongs attached to circles of wire punched through the air with a sound like a metronome cracking as fast as it could go.

It pierced his skin. His body convulsed. His eyes twisted in what I hoped was excruciating pain.

The longest five seconds of my life ticked off like hours. I released the trigger to the taser, the surge of paralyzing electricity stopping immediately. My lungs released a huge gulp of air I hadn't been aware I'd been holding, as thick beads of sweat trailed down my lower back.

The buzzing stopped, and he was right back up again, unphased by the electricity and more crazed than before. Staring straight into his squinted eyes, ignoring my blurred vision, a tremble building in my hands, and the lump growing in my throat, I came up with a new plan.

I gripped the trigger to the taser again, electricity locking his body in place. He fell like dead timber. Without flinching or wavering my grip, I seized my tripod with my free hand and lifted it over my head. Bellowing a warrior's cry, I smashed it down, full force, making a cracking thud against his skull.

An anguished groan escaped his drooling lips. Blood bloomed from the deep gash, drowning his face in liquid red. I lifted the tripod overhead once more and slammed it against his rib cage.

He was immobilized and gravely wounded. It was my chance to run. But, as long as he was able to hunt me down, I wasn't going to stop.

I tossed the taser aside and balled my hands into tight fists, kicking him in the groin with a violence that astonished me. I wanted to maim him, to ensure, if at all possible, he was never able to harm another woman as he intended to harm me.

He curled into the fetal position, whimpering in pain, and I sucked snot down into my throat and swallowed. Raising my left leg once again, I stomped his face. Gathering my camera equipment and purse with trembling hands, I kicked him in the back of the head with my heal in one final blow.

CHAPTER TWENTY

"**9**11 Emergency."
    I locked myself in the news car, 911 on the line, holding a shaky cigarette to my lighter.

"Hi." My voice sounded cold, I didn't know what to say. Gazing out into the late afternoon's dauting red sky, I watched the winter sun wield its final burst of energy, reds and pinks colliding before dissolving into the twilight. "A man attacked me, I need the police. It's 2121 Long Horse Road, Grants Pass."

I narrowed my eyes at the house. My lungs burned and my legs felt weak.

"Are you in a safe place right now?" the woman asked me.

"Yes, I'm locked in my car. He's inside the house, I hit him on the head. I don't know how badly he's hurt."

"Are you injured?"

"I don't know. I think I'm fine."

"What's your name, ma'am?"

My name? I didn't want the world to find out. At least not until the police positively identified the man inside as the murderer on Belle Street and I could go home without worrying about the killer following me.

But it was time to face the facts. I looked at my face in the mirror, covered in who knows who's blood. *I'm sorry, Shelbs*, I thought to myself. *You're not going to be able to keep this one secret.*

With shaking fingers, I took a long drag on my cigarette. "Shelby Rosenberg." I exhaled, using my real last name in a last-ditch effort at anonymity.

It was pointless. A local television reporter had been assaulted on the job. Attempted rape. Ninety percent chance she'd identified a murderer. This was way bigger news than when Jack and I got roughed up on the Alice in Wonderland trail.

My hair lay matted and a mess. Mascara streaked down my smudged face. Still, as I gently twisted from side to side taking in every angle, I couldn't spot a single bruise. Assuming they were still too distracted to follow social media, I could hide this from my parents for a few more weeks. At least until Dad would be near the end of his recovery and hopefully the police would know for sure this guy was the killer.

While the operator did whatever she was doing on the other line, I texted Jack my location and told him I'd been attacked.

Three messages were all he sent back, the first things he'd said to me in the past three weeks:

Jack: Call 911.

Jack: Stay Safe.

Jack: I'm coming for you.

He still cared. We still had a chance.

"They're on their way," I texted Jack while I answered the dispatcher's questions. Grants Pass was a small town, it didn't have its own government-sponsored police or fire department. Even with the cops coming as fast as they could, it may be a while.

I returned to taking inventory of my injuries. I may not have had any noticeable bruises on my face, but the rest of my body felt crushed. My left elbow throbbed. My ribcage felt broken. It hurt to suck in oxygen.

What if Russell wakes up? I felt a new rumble of alarm. I wiped his blood off my forehead and tried to believe he was in no condition to hurt me again. But on instinct, I braced my hand around the steering wheel. I'd wedge him between the car and his house if I had to.

"Shelby, can you see the man who attacked you?" the dispatcher asked, her voice muddled with concern and comfort.

I'd left the front door to the house open. Scanning the entrance I confirmed Russell hadn't moved, I noticed the dog lay motionless as well. Neither of them was going anywhere.

"I can see him through the door, he's still on the ground," I answered, hugging my arm around my aching chest. The fear receded and I willed myself to go numb to any sensations other than the physical pain reminding me I'd survived.

The dispatcher, Joan, a younger sounding woman, stayed on the line with me, promising to talk with me until the police came. Once I'd answered all of her questions, we made small talk. We focused on trivial things, new Netflix shows we were watching, her dating life. Joan was my age, divorced, with two daughters.

The hurried squeal of tires screeching to a halt on wet

asphalt peeled through my ears. I swung my head around as a white pickup truck flew through the empty road. It was Jack.

I rolled my window down, calling for him as he flew out of the truck. From across the street I could see the worry drenching his face. He ran to the news car.

I unlocked it long enough for him to rip my door open and wrap his arms around me. Tears of relief filled my eyes. I was all right. I was a survivor.

"Oh, my God, Shelby." He pressed his cold, trembling hands against my cheeks, wiping the dried blood from my face. "Are you hurt, what happened?"

Jack jangled his keys nervously in his hands. He walked around to the passenger side, climbed in and locked the door. I leaned over and he folded me in his arms. Crumpled in his embrace, I curled my head into his lap. Jack's grip was tender, but as he rubbed my back, his body went rigid.

"I was so scared, Jack." I cried onto his chest, the powerful adrenalin rush flushing clear of my veins, leaving me weak. I pushed myself away far enough to look into his eyes. "I thought I was okay. I had my taser."

Peering over at Russell King's motionless body, Jack said, "that guy looks twice your size, Shelbs, he could've killed you. What were you thinking coming all the way out here alone?" His hand cupped the side of my hand in a frightened rage. "How long has he been out? Is he alive?"

"I don't know." I sniffled. "I think so."

The Dispatcher chimed in over speaker phone, again asking if we were all right, how Russell looked, and re-minded us that the police were only a few minutes away. I couldn't imagine how fast Jack had to drive to get to me so quickly.

He smoothed out my hair. "Who is he?" His face contorted in anguish.

I filled him in on all the details. "This is probably the guy, Jack. He said he wanted to hurt me the way Melissa Rossi was hurt."

Jack held me tighter and I dug my fingertips into his sides for security. "I was doing my job."

Jack arranged himself in the chair, pulling it back so I wasn't wedged between his body and the glove compartment. He turned to keep watch on the house, still peering in the door.

CHAPTER TWENTY-ONE

"**D**o you want me to get you something else from the cafeteria?" Jack sat beside me in a sleek pleather recliner, his forehead knitted in pensive concern.

A golden moon illuminated the inky evening sky outside my private hospital room's large window, as a modern analogue clock on the wall ticked the time; 7:45. I stretched out in the white bed and picked at some bruised fruit on the plastic tray resting on my lap. It'd been at least seven hours since I last touched food. My tummy demanded sustenance.

"I'm getting ready to take a bite." I twisted my lips with distaste at the unappetizing fruit. "How are you doing, Jack?"

"I'm not the one in a hospital bed."

I stabbed my fork into a brown slice of banana, feeling bad he was trapped here with me. Jack had experienced enough trauma in his lifetime. Hospitals couldn't be his favorite place.

But if I were being truly honest with myself, I knew it wasn't being stuck in a hospital that was bothering Jack, it was that he was here with me. The woman who had betrayed him.

"You don't have to stay if you don't want to, Jack. I'm all right. No broken bones or internal ruptures. No major psychological trauma. It's all good."

Jack didn't respond.

"The doctors couldn't find anything." Scans had revealed some torn cartilage in between my ribs and there was a nice goose-egg sized lump on the back of my head. My knee required a few stiches. But nothing serious.

"You should see the other guy." I laughed at my lame cliché, trying to fill the awkward silence. "Seriously ,Jack, I'm all right. You can take off if you want to go home."

I pinched another grape between my fingers to test its plumpness. "My mom called while you were out getting coffee," I continued to babble on, "she booked a flight for tomorrow morning. The station manager called her and told her what happened. She asked for your number so you could pick her up at the airport. I hope that's okay. I didn't want to tell her you weren't really hanging out with me much anymore."

"I'm here now, aren't I?" He stared down at his shoes. "I'll pick up your mom."

"Thanks. Also, thank you for convincing the neighbors to take in Russell King's dog."

"Like a half-dead dog would be a hassle anyway." Jack's blue eyes refused to look at me. He stayed seated though, as if he were here for the long haul. "What did Sergeant Dunbar say to you about all this?" he asked.

Swallowing the tasteless grape, I said, "He told me 'we have to stop meeting this way'. Then he asked about what happened and took a bunch of pictures of me. Pretty much like the time we were attacked on the Alice in Wonderland trail, only now he has to coordinate things with Josephine County officials since this happened over county lines. I asked him about processing Russell's DNA results and he said they'd already swabbed him. It'll take a few weeks for the results."

"Does Dunbar think this guy's the killer?"

"He can't say. I think he fits the profile though. Same race as the victims, middle aged, impulsive, and he lives within driving distance of the house on Belle Street. Not to mention he's a chef with a grudge and Daphne and Melissa were murdered with a knife." I rustled my bare legs under the stiff sheets. "But, of course, nothing is quick about solving a crime. Even when you're willing to take one for the team."

Jack winced at my nonchalance. I hated feeling like I was causing him pain. Straightening the beads on my bracelet, I inhaled, preparing to address the real problem between us, the unspoken hurt permeating our conversation. "I'm sorry, Jack."

"For what?"

"For what I did to us." My stomach twisted in knots. "Besides being all messed up about what was going on with my dad, I was falling so hard for you, so fast. I wasn't ready and I got scared." Tears welled in my eyes. "I was so wrong."

"Nah, I get it. You don't feel the same as me. I mean, let's be real here. You probably want to shop around, you know, have options, find someone smarter, richer, and better than me."

Tears filled my eyes. "Jack, it's not like that at all."

"Sure." He shrugged.

"Jack, the last thing I want is somebody to take care of me. I don't need any of that. All I've fought for, as far back as I can remember, is to be my own person."

I poked at an apple slice. "Then you came along and I was afraid I'd lose everything I struggled for. It's not that you weren't good enough. It's that you were too good." Tears broke.

"Jack?"

He pushed at the cuticle on his thumb.

"Jack? Can you forgive me? Please."

"Are you serious right now, Shelbs?" He looked into me then, his eyes brimming with resentment.

Shame made it difficult to look back at him. "I'm so sorry."

He nodded, letting his hair cover his face. "What you did really hurts."

My guilt tangled with desperate longing. "You opened up your heart to me and shared your secret past and I betrayed you. I know I messed up bad. I've risked losing the best thing I've ever had."

He looked back up and held my gaze, searching me, his will to resist seeming to crack. My heart flipped with hope.

"I'm glad you're okay, Shelby. I need some time."

"All right," I whispered, pulling my eyes away from him and onto my hands, wishing I could start the entire relationship over again. "I understand."

CHAPTER TWENTY-TWO

Mom and I sat transfixed, watching the big screen television from the comfort of my living room couch. The handsome host of *Good Morning USA* clenched his jaw with seriousness. "Brain Trauma. Perhaps permanent memory loss. That's the latest medical update on the man who allegedly attacked a small-town television reporter in Southern Oregon. Russell King is now considered a suspect in the murders of two young women in their home Halloween night."

Mom and I had already watched the story three times.

She clicked the pause button on the remote and looked at me in wonder. "Shelby, you're famous. Can you believe it?"

My skin tingled with tension at the word famous. None of this felt right. I adjusted the pillows under my head, resenting the stiffness throughout my body as I tried to settle into a comfortable position. "Push play. *Brain trauma,* I want to hear that again."

"The police are going to make a statement tomorrow afternoon," my mother continued, brushing off my request.

"That's really great news," I said, a little worried about what they would say, "but I care more about that sick piece of trash never hurting another woman again."

Mom set down the remote beside a mixed bouquet of pink daisies and red and orange roses that Melissa's family sent to my hospital room. Another large bouquet of white roses mixed with pinecones and tiny red flowers from Daphne's mom rested on the kitchen table. The apartment smelled like Christmas at a candle store.

Mom pulled her glossy blonde hair into a loose ponytail and began gathering our lunch dishes scattered across the coffee table. Even at her most annoying, she had a glow. My mother was the most beautiful woman I knew.

"I meant to tell you," she said, "I ran into your old friend Mira Slava the other day."

"She hated me, she was never my friend."

"Well, she was telling me about her wedding coming up and all her exciting plans for a honeymoon in Kazan."

"Mama, you better not start in on me about marriage."

"Why are you always so capricious? One minute happy and pleasant, and the next, completely defiant." She strode with her hands full of dishes toward the kitchen. "What's so horrible about marriage? Here I am, right by your side when you need me most, and you're making me feel unwelcome."

"I'm sorry, I'm so *insufferable, Mother.* Please, tell me more about Mira Slava's wedding and honeymoon. I'm riveted with suspense."

Mom paced back into the room shaking her head in irritation. "Do you remember when you were only nine and you told me you were glad I smoked all the time because I would die of cancer?"

I rolled my eyes. "And you stuck me in therapy for a year. You've mentioned it once or twice."

"What kind of daughter says that to her mother?"

"One with a lot of seething anger and resentment."

"Or maybe you're spoiled, Shelby, and completely ungrateful." My mom looked around the room. "Where's your broom?"

"In the coat closet." I pointed to the small door in the hallway between the two bedrooms. "You don't think my defiant behavior had anything to do with my environment?" I asked.

Mom grabbed the broom and dustpan and began sweeping the non-existent dust bunnies off the living room floor. "You need a housekeeper. This is ridiculous."

"It's fine Mama, my floors are immaculate."

"Your brother never gave me problems, and he turned out fantastic. So, I guess I'm not such a bad mother."

"Where are you going with all this sweetness and love, Mama? What are you buttering me up for?"

She stopped her cleaning and placed her hand on her slender hip. "I want you to come home."

"Can't you let me recuperate for a day before you lay into me?"

"What do you have left here to prove?"

It was a fair question. After most likely helping solve a major murder investigation, it would be easier to find a reporting gig closer to home. "I'm not trying to prove anything. I'm trying to be happy on my own. Why do you have to push so hard?"

"We're getting tired of your games, Shelby."

"So I can end up like you with two kids at twenty-four? Not going to happen, Mama."

As much as I hated to admit it, we were so much alike at our core. Stubborn, independent women. But she was also different. Mom liked being cared for but would tear your heart out if you made her feel like she needed to be cared for. She preferred the illusion of independence.

"And why would it be so horrible to end up like your mother?" She resumed sweeping, not an ounce of contrition on her pretty face. "Do you know how many women would pull out their teeth to have comforts as good as mine?"

"Then why are you always miserable?"

"I have my good days. Besides, what do you think it will do to your father if you stay here? How can he recover if he's worried sick over you?"

I pulled myself up into the sitting position too quickly and felt the ache along my ribs and limbs as I stretched the muscles. The doctors had declared Dad cancer-free. No chemotherapy. No radiation.

He was the one who'd insisted he was doing well and that I needed to stay here. Mom was simply trying to guilt me into coming home. "I'm going outside."

"And I need to get dressed. Your friend Jack's on his way over soon. We're going out to lunch. It's the least I can do, he's looked out for you so much. Jack's a good man, I like him."

"Of course you're taking him to lunch. What else could I expect?" I groaned, scooching off the couch and hobbling to look for my cigarette pack. Truth be told, I was grateful she liked Jack as much as she did. Especially considering he wasn't the kind of guy she usually pushed on me.

Still, my mom was going to drive me crazy if she didn't

leave town tomorrow as promised. I couldn't stand to imagine what she would say to Jack about me when I wasn't around to hear.

CHAPTER TWENTY-THREE

"Is this Shelby Day?" I could hear the buzz of a sophisticated newsroom in the background; voices, scanners, the tapping of keyboards. "This is Aiden Smith. I'm the executive producer with *Good Morning USA.*"

While Mom was out making friends with Jack, I'd been trying to figure out my next move. That's when the phone had rung.

"Oh, hi!" My fingers trembled with nervous excitement. "This is Shelby. You're my favorite morning show."

"Excellent. I'm calling to ask if you'd be interested in appearing live with us tomorrow morning. Sophia Liu and Darius Jones would love to sit down with you via satellite to chat about your reporting heroics. You are no ordinary small-town television reporter."

The butterflies in my stomach exploded into a fireworks show. A feature story on America's number-one morning show would surely catapult me to a bigger market. They were noticing me, they thought I'd made a positive impact, that I'd done a good job.

This was the kind of life-altering event I'd daydreamed

and rehearsed in my imagination since I was a teenager. For the first time since the murders, I could breathe.

"Yes, thank you. I'd love to," I answered, trying not to sound too eager.

The producer and I agreed he would call my news director here in Ashland to work out the details. *Good Morning USA* wanted to interview me at my station. It would look more official.

I smiled, saying goodbye with my best reporter voice, before collapsing onto the couch in shock. How many hours were left in the day? What would I say on the show? What would I wear?

I texted Mom right away, a smile plastered across my face. With her approval, I could finally tell Dad what had happened with Russell King. How I might've helped solve the crime.

Mom had made up some baloney story about needing some girl time with me. But I hated helping Mom lie to Dad, and there would be no way to hide a high-profile, national interview from him. I dragged my sore body to my bedroom to lay out clothes when I began to contemplate the new reality.

Of course, my anxious mind got busy dredging up every possible doomsday scenario. Was I really ready for the bigs? What if I landed a job in LA, and then went live on-air reporting about something historical like the 9/11 attacks and I completely froze? What if I had a full-blown panic attack on camera and slurred my speech so terribly the news director fired me for appearing drunk on camera? I'd only worked as a television reporter for eleven months, not even one full year. I wasn't ready for something like this.

Or, what if Russell King wasn't the killer?

Chills coursed through my body and my hands tingled, going numb. *No*, I scolded myself. *Stop it, Shelby. Stop catastrophizing.* It's not like I was actually going on air to say I'd led police to the murderer. We didn't have confirmation on Russell King, and I would handle any new job opportunity I earned with grace.

My phone chimed. A text came through. It was Mom.

Mom: Your dad called. The doctors got some new labs back that don't look good. They're saying it looks like your dad still has cancer. A more aggressive treatment is necessary.

Just like that, my confidence evaporated. Nothing was going to be fine. My dad's health was back on the line. Worse than before. I needed to go home— immediately.

CHAPTER TWENTY-FOUR

My head pounded with urgency. I had to talk to the police. If Russell King wasn't the killer, I could be luring a monster back to my family.

The second Mom and Jack returned home from lunch, I told her I had to run errands to get ready for my sit-down with *Good Morning USA.*

"I'll come with you." Mom scooted her red purse strap back onto her shoulder, looking resolved to heading back out into the cold.

I didn't have time to argue with her and there was no way I was bringing her with me. "Why don't you pack up for your flight in the morning and take a nap. It's going to be a long day tomorrow and you don't want to look haggard when you get home. You never know what celebrities you might bump into at LAX."

Mom fidgeted with her purse strap. Whether she admitted it or not, I knew I had pushed the right button. "Bring Jack with you. I don't want you running around alone."

I didn't want to take Jack either, but it was quicker to

agree to her terms. "Jack?" I asked, reaching into the coat closet for a jacket. "Do you mind?"

"Sure." He shrugged.

As soon as we climbed into the Escalade, before I clicked open the garage door, I told him the truth. "I'm heading to the Ashland Police department."

"Why?"

"I know I said that creep who tried to hurt me was the killer, but the truth is, I'm not one-hundred-percent certain. I need to find out if there's anything Dunbar's holding back."

Jack pursed his lips.

"I'm moving back to Los Angeles," I told Jack as if it meant nothing, "but I can't leave town without knowing for sure this case is solved. If Russell King isn't the one, the real murderer could follow me home."

Jacks right hand tightened into a fist. "Why would you think that?"

"Because I got another note from the stalker a few weeks ago. Before you say anything, I didn't tell you because you weren't speaking to me at the time, and also I didn't want to upset you. But basically, the note said if I got any closer to solving the crime, he or she would come after me."

His jaw pulsed with tension. "Why would anyone do that?"

"Do what?" I asked.

"If you leave, you're out of the picture. End of story. Why do you think your stalker would come after you? It doesn't make sense."

Relieved he didn't freak out on me about keeping the note a secret, I answered his question. "Killers aren't rational,

Jack. I don't want to be looking over my shoulder for the rest of my life." I jammed the key into the ignition and opened my nearly soundless garage door. Dull sunlight slunk inside the dim garage.

"If the killer's really stalking you," Jack continued, "and it's not just some random leaving scary notes on your door, don't you think it'll make him even angrier to see you poking around the police department?"

Throwing the car in reverse, I backed up the SUV. "I can drop you off at your place first if you want, Dunbar's more likely to talk to me if I'm alone."

"Risking your safety to solve the crime is all about your fame, isn't it?" he spat.

I wasn't prepared for him to be so mean. "If you think I'm such a rotten person, why do you worry so much about me?"

He shot me a dirty look. "So once you're sure Russell King is the killer, you're taking off? Right? That's it?"

I popped my sunglasses out of their overhead compartment and slid them on. "So that's what you're pissed off about."

He stared straight ahead. Dead silence.

"My dad isn't cancer-free like we thought, Jack. My mom probably didn't say anything because she's super private about family issues. But now that they know I've been attacked, it would worry my dad too much if I stayed. He'll figure I've come close enough to solving the case and it's no longer worth sticking around. I can't risk him not recovering because of me." I turned away from Jack, a heaviness settling into my chest. "I don't want to leave, though, until we fix things between you and me. I meant what I said about not wanting to lose you. Maybe that's the real reason I'm so unsure, the reason I'm stalling out and questioning if

Russell King really is our guy. I want an excuse to stay. But I also have to think about my dad's health." Tears of frustration pooled in my eyes. Everything was happening at once and far too quickly.

Jack looked frozen, poker-faced. "Family first. Always. I'll wait for you in the lobby."

Exiting the alley, I flicked on my right turn signal and prepared to pull onto the main road. *Solve one problem at a time, Shelby. First things, first.* I'd talk to Sergeant Dunbar, then I'd figure out what to do next.

Jack clicked on his seatbelt. "This isn't a good idea."

———

After making us sit and wait a good thirty minutes, the receptionist, sporting a crisp white button-down dress shirt and a crew cut, called me through the wooden doors. He didn't have to, but he reminded me that Sergeant Dunbar's desk was at the back of the office. When I stepped inside, it was easy to spot the six-foot-three detective standing behind the blinds in his side office. He was one of only a handful of officers occupying the space that Tuesday afternoon, and his smooth head towered over most of his seated colleagues.

"Shelby Day, good to see you." He sat down in front of his computer monitor and rubbed his hand across his mustache. "Sit down, what can I do for you?"

The radio on his desk hissed, a woman's voice buzzed from behind it, "10-42, Sergeant Amarissa Quezada, That's a 10—"

Sergeant Dunbar took the radio, turned it down and

clipped it to his belt. "Ignore that, it's just the radio. What do you need?"

"You sure you don't want to answer that?"

"It goes out to everybody. What can I do for you?"

I pulled up the giant wooden seat in front of his desk. "There's something I forgot to mention before we hung up. It's important." I reached into my purse for the most recent anonymous note I'd received and smoothed it out on his desk. "I found this taped on my front door about three weeks ago."

Sergeant Dunbar put his half-moon glasses on, squinting at the paper on his desk, holding it down with the edge of his pen, careful not to touch the paper with his fingers.

I'm still here.
This Ms. Day, is your final warning.
Do you want to live for another morning?

He took a sip of coffee, the words *Sunriver, Oregon* printed on the side, his face tensed with a look of genuine concern. "He likes to rhyme."

"No doubt." I crossed my legs, trying to keep my left foot from bouncing in anxiety. "Maybe he writes children's books."

"Shelby, why are you coming to me with this now? Did you put up security cameras or report the notes like I told you? You've found yourself in enough trouble as it is."

His advice only made me want to dig deeper. "I don't know what to do."

"Would you like to file a report on the note?"

The radio buzzed again, this time a man's voice hissed something from Dunbar's hip.

"I'd rather make sure we've found the killer, then the note won't feel so threatening." I leaned in closer. "It's been over a month since the murders on Belle Street. You've interviewed hundreds of potential witnesses. Do you think it's Russell King, and if not, what's next?"

"Shelby," Sergeant Dunbar pushed his glasses over his eyes and began typing on his computer.

"Do you think we've got him?" My stomach felt like I'd swallowed rocks. I had to be sure my family and I were safe before I went home.

"You know I can't comment on an active investigation."

Thank goodness I'd spent most of my adult life studying criminal minds. I'd transitioned from *Dateline*'s stories to true-crime podcasts and murder mystery novels. I was familiar with the tricks of the trade. "Investigators always hold something back, some piece of information only the killer would know so if someone calls in and falsely claims they did it, you can find out if they're telling the truth or not."

"And?"

"There're still other options you haven't turned over. What about Daphne's secret fiancé's estranged wife? She had reason to want Daphne dead. Did you talk with her?"

"I can't share that information."

"Julien told me no one called his ex."

"You're not going to get anything out of me, Shel-bee." Sergeant Dunbar hummed, wiggling his mouse while typing on the computer. He reminded me of my dad, trying to let me down in the kindest way possible.

I continued talking. "The victims' families and friends opened up to me in ways they may not have with the cops. Maybe if I knew your secret piece of the puzzle, whatever little details you're holding back, I could help you guys, too. Look how much I've accomplished so far all on my own."

"If you want to do the detective work, I can give you an application." He pushed back in his black leather business chair. "But, until you get out of the academy, I'm happy to make you a third copy of all of the media releases. You're welcome to sift through them. I'll even put them in a binder for you this time."

"I've read through all that information a thousand times already, Sergeant."

"I don't know what to tell you, Ms. Day. I can't give you anything else."

"What about a tiny hint? What about laying the file on your desk and having the fan *accidentally* blow it over when you get an emergency call and need to walk away?"

"Shelby, you've got guts, I'll tell you that much." He chuckled. "What you're insinuating is illegal. This isn't some crime show, it doesn't work that way."

He wasn't taking me seriously, I could feel the stress gripping my insides. "All right, I'll stop bothering you. I'll take the copies of the media releases. Maybe I missed something."

"Sure thing, Kiddo."

The only person who seemed to believe in my ability to solve this crime for certain was the douchbag leaving notes on my door. "What if this guy tries to hurt me?" I asked.

Sergeant Dunbar sighed, picked up his cell, typed something into it, and held it to his ear.

"What are you—" My phone buzzed. I furrowed my brow, picking up the phone. "Sergeant Dunbar?"

"Ah, so it does work." He chuckled. "If you feel like you're in danger, call us as soon as you can."

He swiveled around to the commercial-sized printer behind his desk.

"Thank you, Sergeant." I eyed the computer screen tilted away from my vision, the one he said he would never leave turned on for me to view like they do in the movies.

"I like you, Shelby. You've got a strong sense of justice." The printer's motor whirred as it prepared to shoot out warm press releases. "I'm sure there are plenty of bigger markets interested in hiring you, but we like you here in Ashland."

The radio on his desk hissed, "Sergeant Dunbar, we have a 10-10 at 1475 Siskiyou Blvd. We're going to need you over here."

"I gotta run." Dunbar reached over to his desk, making eye contact with me as he turned off his computer. "Come on, I'll walk you outside."

I had to do something big. Time was running out. Find the missing clue or risk the possibility of spending the rest of my life worrying about a killer coming after me.

If only I could rip through the files on his computer. I looked at him, my eyes pleading, showing him my desperation. "So there's nothing you're holding back that you—"

"Grab your things, Shelby." He spoke with authority. "I'll walk you outside."

I leaned over to pick up my purse and noticed my phone had fallen on the floor, halfway underneath the backside of his desk.

———

I waved at Sergeant Dunbar as he jogged to his police car, sirens blazing before he even took off. I pulled out and circled around the street before darting back in front the station.

"What are you doing?" Jack asked.

"Wait here. I'll be right back."

He put his hand on my shoulder as I released the seat belt. "Come on, Shelbs, let it go."

"I can't, Jack. I owe it to those women and to myself. I can drive you home really quick and drop you off, but I know you. You're going to stick by my side. So why not skip the arguing?"

He removed his hand from my shoulder in defeat.

"Stay here." I shivered as I stepped back out of the Escalade and wrapped my black scarf around my neck.

This was it. My final opportunity for a bold move.

CHAPTER TWENTY-FIVE

Jack looked at me with narrowed eyes as I climbed back into the Escalade. "Well?"

I turned up the heat in the running car and poked around my purse for a cigarette. "I told the newbie officer at the front desk I'd left my cell phone behind. Poor guy, he kept dropping his pen and looking really nervous. He walked me into the main floor of the department to find it. I thought I could sneak on Sergeant Dunbar's computer somehow or go through his file folders, but the guy wouldn't leave me alone."

"So, it's over."

I put a cigarette in my mouth and flicked the lighter, running the flame over the tip as I inhaled. "Want one?" I asked, blowing a stream of blue-white smoke sideways out the cracked-open window as I spoke.

Jack shook his head.

"I struck up a conversation with him. I told him I'd been there to talk Sergeant Dunbar about Russell King, how I still, you know, wasn't sure he was right guy."

"Yeah?"

"He looked really nervous, so I asked him if he wanted to share a cigarette break. He said he didn't smoke, but he laughed when he saw I offered him Camel Turkish Golds."

"Since when do you smoke anything besides American Spirit?"

"Since this is what they happened to have left at the convenience store." I waved him off. "Anyway, the officer asked me if Russell King was a smoker. I told him I had no idea, and then he mentioned they found a pile of Camel Turkish Gold cigarettes butts beside the women's garage the night of the murders. Then the officer got this nervous laugh. I asked what was so funny, he said 'w-well, Sergeant Dunbar said you were a really good investigator.' I didn't know what he was talking about, but I wasn't about to let that go, ya know? So I said 'Oh yeah, I bought these right after the murders to help me get closer to the case'. He said, 'You've got guts to try to get closer to the murderer like that'. I went out on a limb and said 'I walked outside the house afterwards, looking for clues the police would've missed' and he said 'We only found the glass from the broken windows and a pile of cigarette butts by the garage where we assume the killer chain-smoked before the murder.'"

"Total creeper."

"That's not the point!" I almost jumped in the seat out of excitement. "That must be the secret piece of information."

"Huh?"

"The killer smoked Camel Turkish Gold cigarettes. He chain-smoked and left his butts all over the ground the night he killed Daphne and Melissa."

"And that means . . . ?"

"I don't know. I was hoping for something better."

"Do you remember if Russell King smelled like cigarettes the day, you know?" Jack looked out the window. "The day you fought him off."

"No. He told me he didn't smoke. But people lie about stuff like that."

"Did the officer say anything else?"

"He asked for my Instagram."

"So he was trying to hit on you."

"He was definitely trying to impress me. I'm going to hit him up on social media and chat with him, see what else I can find out. Crew Cut's got a big mouth. I bet I can get him to talk."

I dropped Jack off and drove home, pondering the possibilities. The young officer was a gift I was going to unwrap—fast.

CHAPTER TWENTY-SIX

I sat stiff-backed, my underarms damp with perspiration, in an overstuffed purple chair on the morning set of *NBC 4 News*. Clipping on the mic lavalier, I inserted my custom-molded IFB into my ear so I could hear from the director's booth.

Both my news director and the station owner had come in before our station's early show began to sit in the director's booth. Mom had found a spot in the newsroom with Jack and our assignment editor. They were all here to watch my live interview with *Good Morning USA*.

I squinted into the camera. The overhead spotlight hurt my eyes as they adjusted to the artificial brightness.

"Let's get a sound check." Our morning director's voice rang clear in my earpiece.

"One. Two. Three. Check. Check. Ch—"

"You're good, Shelby."

The morning show's executive producer told us they would focus on my assault by Russell King while out investigating potential suspects for the Belle Street murders. That was, as long as I agreed to state on-air that I took full responsibility for going alone into a potential double homicide suspect's home without anyone from the newsroom's permission. *NBC 4 News* was a sister station for *Good Morning USA*—I had to make them look good.

Of course, Mom had to be upset about something. She said taking responsibility for the Russell King attack weakened my chances of winning a future lawsuit against NBC or its affiliate. Ignoring the knot in my stomach over once again having to deal with my upset mother, I told myself that taking responsibility was for the best. It wasn't the station's fault that I snuck out alone.

Even if it was, I wasn't going to go sue-crazy over it. This was my chance to build a career, make a name for myself. Taking the sister station for *Good Morning USA* to court was a great way to get blackballed from the news industry for life.

None of that would even matter, however, if I didn't pull off something dramatic. Mom's flight to Los Angeles was leaving in a few hours and we'd already told my dad about Russell King and this interview. Dad was scared. The clock was ticking. I'd promised him I would follow Mom home, I had to. Everything that mattered was slipping out of my control. The case, Jack; everything was falling away.

From the beat-up black and white fifteen-inch television monitor placed next to the looming, mounted studio camera, I watched on close caption as *Good Morning USA's* Sophia Liu introduced my story and played a full pre-recorded piece on the events leading up to my interview with them.

"Stand by," my director spoke into my earpiece, the tension thick in his command.

If I couldn't solve this case, or fix things with Jack, I could at the very least share something so dramatic that I would surely be able to land an on-air position in a big market close to home.

Think, Shelby, think. I'd rehearsed this all night, not to mention I'd spent years interning in college studying my craft. I'd prepared all my life to make my mark on the news world. I had to be able to come up with something.

This interview was my last chance to salvage my career—the only thing I may have left at this point. I watched Sophia and her co-anchor, Darius Jones, exchange serious expressions as they faced the camera and told viewers I was live via satellite in Ashland, Oregon.

"And standby . . ."

The muscles in my back tensed. Our floor director operating the live camera pointed his index finger at me. I felt short of breath as I warmed into a sweat, pools forming in my armpits. Deep anxiety set in, clouding my head and shaking my core. The beginning signs of a panic attack.

I drew in a shaky breath, I'd done plenty of live interviews, I was fine. This whole thing would be over in three to four minutes.

Ticktock. My brain scrambled to work harder. "Thank you for having me, Sophia and Darius."

Sophia Liu, with her cropped black hair and bright red lips, looked so poised and professional it made me question my own reporting skills. Surely if she were in my shoes, she'd know exactly what to do.

She leaned in toward the camera, her manicured hands neatly folded on her lap, and asked me the first question. "Shelby, what was going through your mind when the

Grants Pass restaurateur allegedly lunged at you?"

I drew in a breath, pushing my nerves to the side, speaking clearly and eloquently. Dad would be proud.

"I wasn't really thinking anything. He was a big guy and I was there alone. I needed to get out, that's all I could think about. I had to defend myself."

"How do you mean defend yourself?" she asked.

"I had a taser in my camera bag. When he turned to attack I lunged for it. I wasn't quick enough."

"What happened next?" Darius Jones, a former basketball star, with the long legs to prove it, tilted his head to the side with concern.

I pushed a lock of my hair off my forehead, feeling my sweat bubbling under the heat of the lamps in the studio. No time to blot it now. I drew in another breath.

"He jumped on top of me and tried to assault me. Russell King tried to take advantage of somebody that he thought was weaker than he was. He really underestimated me, he didn't think I'd fight back. A lot of people have asked me about him, all I can say is that he got what he deserved and everything that happened is because of the choices that he made."

"How were you able to react so quickly?"

I knew enough about this industry to know she probably wasn't all that concerned, but she hid it well behind her perfectly shaped eyebrows.

"I took boxing lessons with my dad." I grinned. "My friend made sure I carried a taser. It helped save me."

Darius crossed his legs. "This was the second time you've been attacked in the last three weeks."

My palms went damp with sweat, I could hear the blood

pumping in my ears. "That is correct. I'm very fortunate my dad enrolled me in boxing courses when I was little." I joked, hoping to change the subject. My parents still didn't know about the first attack.

"We understand two men hid on a bike trail and assaulted you and a friend before stealing your grandmother's wedding ring from your finger. You were knocked unconscious."

I could feel the blood draining from my face. My lips began to quiver. Dad was watching. This revelation could push his anxiety so high he'd never recover.

I flashed a smile for the camera, I couldn't think of that right now. I couldn't let my nerves ruin this chance I had at my dream. "It's been a rough few weeks. No doubt. Both those men were sentenced to three months in prison."

"Did you ever think journalism could be so dangerous?"

"Dangerous?" I pulled back my shoulders and hid a cleansing breath behind a starlight laugh. "As an investigative reporter, my mission is to ask the tough questions and dig deep. I will certainly be smarter about my decisions in the future, and I encourage others to keep aware of their surroundings. But I will always look for new angles and push relentlessly to bring criminals to justice. That's my job. I take it seriously."

Sophia nodded. "So, it was your decision to go inside that man's house alone? You thought the story was worth it?"

There it was. My mandatory opportunity to give the station what they wanted, to agree it was my choice and nobody else's. "Yes, it was my decision to follow this story. It was against the rules of the *NBC 4* station. It was my choice, my mistake. I wanted to get that story so badly, but

I never thought I was risking my life for it. I've definitely learned my lesson, I will never take on anything alone like that again. I think it's very important for people going into this industry to understand that your safety is more important than the story."

Seemingly satisfied, Sophia moved on. "Before we introduced you, we ran a news feature on the two young women who were murdered in their home while they slept on Halloween night. We understand you've been the lead reporter on this investigation, and that's why you drove out to Russell King's house in the first place. You thought he may have been related to the crime in some way. What have you learned?"

"I've become extraordinarily invested in this tragedy after getting to know the victims through their families and friends. Daphne Deluca and Melissa Rossi were special girls. Their parents deserve to know why this happened to their daughters. Unfortunately, police are waiting on DNA evidence, so we can't be sure of anything yet."

My legs felt weak and my eyes went blurry. Licking the salt from lips, my head began to buzz. Time slowed to a near stop. I desperately needed a cigarette.

In the split seconds that ticked on as Sophia waited for me to continue, I remembered each of my interviews, my brain homing in on the clues that had been there all along. Shivers ran down every inch of my body.

The truth hit me like a knife slashing through my flesh. I was nearly certain I knew who the killer was. I could see the secret.

"Shelby? Shelby are you still with us." Sophia Lui's smooth voice sounded in my ear.

"Yes, yes, I'm sorry. I temporarily lost hearing in our connection. It's good now."

"You were telling us what you've learned so far in your investigation."

I exhaled, almost in a laugh, I knew who it was. My lips spread in a shaky smile, "I can't reveal anything yet, but I've uncovered some facts I think will be instrumental in solving the case. I plan on going to the police with everything I know very soon."

The revelation escaped my mouth before I had time to stop myself. I could feel my face redden with panic, but I maintained that starlight smile for the camera.

"That's wonderful news." Sophia smiled. "Everybody must be right about you, Shelby Day. You sure are one of Ashland's up and coming news reporters."

"Yes, thank you." I wanted that to excite me, but the thought of the last note on my door clouded my brain.

This Ms. Day, is your final warning. Do you want to see another morning?

Sophia continued. "You'll have to join us again when you can tell us more."

My upper lip trembled. "Absolutely. I'd be honored to talk with you."

"In the meantime," Darius advised, "better get back in that boxing ring and work on your moves."

Like an absolute cheeseball, my left hand instinctually tightened into a fist and I threw a fake punch at Darius. "Fast and furious."

My heartbeat throbbed in my chest. I pulled my hand

down from my air punch, fist still clenched in front of my chest, and smiled, beaming at myself in the reflection of the news monitor. I remembered my first boxing lesson, gazing at myself in the wall length gym mirror, my dad kneeling behind me, hands on my shoulders, encouraging me from behind, "Shelby, there are two rules in boxing. Never act like you're going to finish a fight until it's over. And keep your guard up. Never, never behave as if you're not afraid of your enemy."

The killer had to be after me. Would Melissa and Daphne's murderer catch me before I reached the police?

CHAPTER TWENTY-SEVEN

I took my time undoing my clipped mic and taking out my IFB. I needed a plan. I had to get rid of my mother. Immediately.

She would murder me herself if she got me alone when I walked off the set. Mom would be furious I didn't wait to get home before letting the entire country know I had secret knowledge about the murderer on Belle Street. I'd put myself in danger for a dream that, in her mind, was ridiculously unnecessary. To her, building a career was a passing fascination that would fade. She could never understand how important it was for me to stand on my own, how much of a privilege it was to find meaning doing something meaningful for others.

"You did great, Shelby," my freckle-faced floor director assured me.

"Thanks, Chip." I let out a long exhale. "Now I have to deal with the real nightmare, my mother."

I stood up with exaggerated slowness and exited the studio into a dark hallway that led to the newsroom.

"Hey," I greeted her, my face no doubt ashen with anxiety.

She paced the pathway between our news desks, her arms crossed tight against her chest. "We need to pack your bags."

"Mom, you can't tell me—"

"Are you a fool, Shelby? Have you lost whatever sense God gave you?" She stopped and stared at me, her eyes wild with anger. "Twice, Shelby. Twice somebody has attacked you. And now you tell the entire world you can put away the vile man who butchered those poor young girls. How could I raise such a *stupid* child? That murderer was watching you, I know it. You made yourself a target."

"Mom—"

"This isn't a debate," she growled, raising her hand to command me to stop. Resentment burned in my gut. "You don't get to decide anymore, Shelby. We're leaving—*you* are leaving. We can hire movers once we're back in LA. You're coming home to rest and recuperate with your father and then we can begin to discuss what's next."

She stepped closer to me, so close I could feel her warm breath on my face. "Do you have any idea what this is going to do to your dad right now?"

Tears of frustration and hurt blurred my vision. "I know that."

"He's sick, Shelby. His state of mind matters. Worrying about his only daughter is going to be the death of him."

I hated my mother for using my dad against me, for acting as if I hadn't already thought of all the things she was throwing at me. "Tell him I'm safe. Go home, and I'll follow you in a few days. A couple more days won't make a difference."

"Don't be selfish. Put your family first for once," she said, her eyes lasering into mine.

Selfish? My self-absorbed, narcissistic mother demanded I throw away everything I'd ever worked for or wanted, and she had the audacity to say I was the one being selfish? I stormed away from her, slamming myself into my desk chair and tying my hair into a tight knot.

Her posture softened as she lost adrenaline. After taking deep breaths and reminding myself I loved her, I decided for the sake of everyone involved to take a gentler approach. She was weakening. I could end this argument.

"*Mamochka*, you already have a plane ticket scheduled for this afternoon. Go and I will leave in a couple of days," I said to pacify her, to get her to leave town. "If you talk to Dad, he will listen to you. He'll calm down. Let me give my news director notice so I can turn over my things. I need to say goodbye to everyone, especially Jack."

This arrangement would give me time to pull all the loose ends together. I would give Sergeant Dunbar my full report. My dad would understand. He'd want me to do this.

As if Jack had been sent as peacemaker, he poked around the corner. "Hey Shelby, great interview."

"Jack, would you mind hanging out with me for the next day or so while I get ready to fly home?"

Scratching the back of his head, he walked toward us. "Sure."

"Mom?" I looked at her for approval.

"What is he going to do?" Mom asked. "Follow your every move? I'm not leaving without you, Shelby." Her face was still rigid.

If I wanted to avoid an explosion, I needed to prove to her I would be safe. "Jack can move in with me and be my bodyguard. I'll turn in my resignation and leave here on good terms, Mama. Maybe all the good work I've done and my interview on *Good Morning USA* will be enough to land a job in Los Angeles."

"Or…" Mom stared into me like a dazzling cougar preparing to crush its prey, "you can pick another project."

I stared right back at her. "This is a career. It is not a project. Not once in my life have you made any effort to truly understand me. Can you help me out? Just this once. I know if you talk to Dad, you'll be able to make him feel better. He always listens to you. I agreed to come home. In a few days. That's my compromise."

She huffed in temporary resignation, striding toward the abandoned assignment desk and seizing her Prada handbag. "Take me straight to the airport. I feel like everyone is listening to us around here. It's not a pleasant environment."

She cruised toward the exit. "Jack, are you coming?"

He fell into step behind us as Mom and I made our reluctant truce. She would leave. Then I would go straight to the police.

Butterflies inside my stomach flapped in anticipation. My future had all come down to the next forty-eight hours.

CHAPTER TWENTY-EIGHT

"I think I know who the killer is," I said, jamming the Escalade into reverse and gunning the engine the moment Jack and I dropped my mom off at the airport. "I'm heading to the Ashland Police department before I go anywhere else."

Jack looked incredulous. "You weren't bluffing in your interview? Why didn't you tell them while you were live?"

"I needed to make sure first," I said, pushing on my sunglasses to block the afternoon glare. "Also, I didn't want to throw the officer I talked to yesterday under the bus. If I told everybody what I knew on national television, he could lose his job. I need to talk directly to Sergeant Dunbar."

"So, who do you think did it?"

"When I was talking with *Good Morning USA,* it all clicked. I remembered my very first interview with Liberty, Melissa's best friend. Her boyfriend, Brandon, had offered me a cigarette. Of course, I checked out the pack. It wasn't the brand I normally smoked.

"The addict in me took in all the details. Brandon drew on his cigarettes with force until they glowed brightly, then he flicked them away and exhaled the smoke.

Chain smoker. Camel Turkish Gold. He'd tossed his cigarettes butts in the dirt, just like that newbie cop told me the killer did on the night of the murders.

Brandon had to have been inside Daphne and Melissa's home at least once before with his fiancée, and would have been able find his way around, including where the girls slept."

Jack pinched the skin at his throat. "Has anybody looked at him as a potential suspect?"

"As far as I know, no one even questioned him."

"What would be his motive?" he asked.

"He's supposed to be getting married in a few weeks. Maybe Brandon was hooking up with Melissa on the side and she threatened to tell Liberty or something. They asked Melissa Rossi's mom to give a speech at their wedding. How sick is that?"

Before I could begin driving again, my phone rang. I checked the caller ID. It read unknown number.

"Are you going to answer it?" Jack asked me.

"It's probably Dunbar." I slid the answer button.

"Congratulations, Shelby." A man's menacing voice slithered out of my Bluetooth car speakers for both Jack and me to hear.

Fear cut through my nerves. "Who is this?"

"You know who it is. It's time we meet up."

I looked over a Jack and put my fingers to my lips to tell him to keep quiet. I had to get the upper hand. "Tell me more. I'm alone."

"Jack is your constant shadow."

My heart stopped. I glanced around the road, looking for somebody, anybody who could be watching me. The voice rang deep in the phone, yanking me back into my twisted reality, "Listen. I've collected someone close to you, someone you wouldn't want to lose. If you want her to keep all her fingers, I'd suggest you stay truthful."

My mind went straight to my mother. I scanned the parking lot looking for her. Jack and I had walked her up to security. How could anyone have hurt her inside the airport with all the TSA there?

"What do you mean collected? Who do you have?" My eyes scoured the parking lot. "My mom? You messed with the wrong woman, she'll beat your ass."

"No." His voice was quiet. Cold. Calculated. Almost as if he was hiding from somebody. "Your friend. The pretty blonde one. Kaya something. I've seen you hang out after work. I need you to listen to me Shelby Day, and listen carefully."

Before I could think, he spoke again. "What happened on the trail, the notes, the dead rose, that was only meant to scare you off the investigation. But you had to act like you were bulletproof, didn't you? Well, now's your chance to be a real hero and save your friend. If you don't do what I say, she'll end up just like Melissa and Daphne."

"Are you stupid or something? I barely even like Kaya, why would I help her?"

Worry knotted in my stomach and I wished I could suck my words back in. Stricken with fear, I had to think fast.

"Wait," I shouted into the speaker.

I couldn't do it, I couldn't leave an innocent girl to die. I had to try. "What do you want me to do?"

Chances were high that if I did what this man asked, it wouldn't save Kaya, just hurt both of us. My lungs constricted and it hurt to breathe. I'd come to Ashland to help people and instead I'd failed on every level.

After what seemed like the longest pause imaginable, he spoke. "So, now we're going to play in the big leagues. It's your life or hers. I'll let her go when you show up."

My skin felt like it'd been lit on fire.

"Go home. You'll find instructions there. No police, you come alone. Be there by eight."

The phone clicked off.

CHAPTER TWENTY-NINE

"I need a plan." I bit off the edges of my thumbnail, trying to push past my terror and think. "Do you want me to drop you off at your place first? You heard him, he made it clear I need to do this alone."

"Are you kidding me right now, Shelby? You're going?" Jack jerked his head back in disbelief.

"Don't you want me to save your precious Kaya?" I spat out in utter fear and frustration, jamming the car into drive, preparing to exit the parking lot onto Maple Street. "I'm heading back to the house to read the note."

Jack adjusted his seat and stared straight ahead. "We should go to the police."

"And say what? He didn't tell us his name, admit who he was or where he was." My brain was so shaken it made it difficult to focus on anything beyond the six-minute drive home. "He's watching us, if we report this, he'll kill Kaya. If he's really the one, he's already murdered two other women."

I pressed my foot harder on the accelerator, made a sharp right onto North Main Street and flew past the handful of cars on the road, all while Jack called Kaya's cell phone, texted her roommate, and checked to see if she'd come into work. I took a swift left on Hersey and about a minute later, came to a squealing stop in the ally beside my yellow apartment's front door. A white note flapped in the cold wind.

"Did she go into work?" I asked as he tapped the phone in thought.

His eyebrows knitted in worry. "Carolyn told me Kaya texted in sick. Kaya's roommate said she last saw her when she was getting in her car on her way to work. So far nobody seems to have made the connection that she's missing."

My pulse raced harder. "You didn't tip them off, did you? If someone calls the police, he'll kill her, Jack. I'm sure of it." Heat flashed through my body, sweat dampening my lower back as dark menacing clouds stacked in suffocating layers across a dull gray sky.

"I didn't let on to anything." He flung his phone onto the floor of the car like he wanted to annihilate it. "This is insane."

"Stay put." Leaving the Escalade running, I rushed the front door and ripped off the note.

Jack rolled down his window. "What does it say?"

Scrawled on the paper was a heart, in it was a brief message that read:

"Why the heart? Where is this place?" I asked, my hands beginning to shake. Jack led me inside and sat me down on the couch, drawing all of the curtains in the living room.

"It's a lake down in Northern California right below the border. In a remote area, it's a long hike to the punchbowl."

"But why there? Why so far away?"

"Gives him time to prepare. He's probably into hiking, this is most likely somewhere he's familiar with."

"Great, so there's another advantage he has over me."

Stricken with fear, I began pacing the living room.

"What time is it?" I asked.

"It's 12:30." Jack pursed his lips. "We'll never make it in time. It's a two-and-a-half-hour drive to a six-mile hike. They close it for winter. Snow's probably covering the switchbacks."

I strode back and forth across the hardwood floor. "Do you have a gun for hunting?"

"Why?"

"Why do you think, Jack? This guy's murdered two other girls, I'm not going to be a third, and Kaya isn't either if I've got anything to say about it. I'm tired of him having the upper hand. And you know what else?" I said, high on manic adrenaline and revving into my instinct to fight. "He's nothing. He's some coward who killed two women in their sleep, not even man enough to do it when they had a fighting chance. I'm not going to let him hurt anybody else."

"So that's your plan?" Jack's mouth nearly fell open. "You're going to march out on the trail and kill him?"

"If he tries to hurt me, I'll do what I have to do." I asked. "Do you have a rifle?"

He nodded in confirmation.

"Then I'll hide it in the waistline of my pants," I answered with confidence, pulling my old backpack out of my coat closet and filling it with water bottles. "Somebody is watching us, we can't call the police. They're never going to be able to sneak out there in time to save her."

"Shelbs?" Jack said softly, as if he was trying to hold his patience with me. "A hunting rifle won't fit in your pants."

I swore in frustration, the edge of my confidence already beginning to wane. I knew next to nothing about guns. The closest I got was when I ran with a tagging crew. I wasn't even a real gang-banger, I used my fists for everything.

"Who would help that guy out, anyway? Who would do that?" Jack asked.

"I don't know. He got two guys to beat the crap out of us already on the Wonderland Trail. He probably has Liberty or another one of his buddies keeping an eye on us. If I don't go there alone, they'll tell him to kill Kaya and make a run for it."

"How? I don't even think that there's cell service out there."

"Maybe he's got a sat phone."

"Then he's gonna have to adjust his plans because I'm going with you. Besides, he's probably going to be packing, too. He'll see you coming and make you put up your hands. Then he'll find the gun."

Again, Jack made a good point.

"You don't even know how to use one. I never got the chance to take you to the range," he dug further.

"How hard can it be to point and shoot? I used the taser just fine."

He shook his head in disbelief. "I've got a handgun, but there's no way you're going alone. You'd never survive the trek out there and, even if you did, it'd be a whole lot easier to ambush the dude if there were two of us."

I zipped up the pack and rubbed my sweaty hands on my jeans. Jack was right. As much as I didn't want to drag him into my mess, or increase the chances of getting Kaya killed, there was no way I could pull this off alone. "I guess we have to risk his accomplice telling him we're together. It's not like I called the police on him."

I bit at my lower lip, recalibrating the plan in my head. When we got close to the Devils Punchbowl, I'd have Jack fall behind. Brandon, or whoever the killer was, might have been watching me close enough all this time to know Jack would never leave my side, but that didn't mean he'd be able to spot Jack right away. Jack could sneak up from behind with the gun. I'd take my taser just in case, tucked in my waistband the way I wanted to do with a gun. If I got a chance, I'd paralyze my stalker. "Let's go Jack," I said, carting my backpack filled with water and food.

"Hold on, Shelby." Jack looked at the screen of his phone. "It'll be dark by 5 o'clock. We'll have to bring more than that. Flashlights, hiking shoes, warm clothes, waterproof jackets, and hiking poles. It's a trek."

Contemplating his list, I raced toward my bedroom closet for the hiking boots I'd never worn. "I don't have all that stuff. We need to just hurry and go."

Jack followed behind me. "Grab what you can and we'll get the rest at my place. This is a gnarly hike, Shelby. When the sun sets, the temperatures drop below freezing. Who knows what we'll find when we get there."

It was bad enough Kaya had been dragged into my mission to solve the crime. If anything happened to Jack, I wasn't sure I could recover.

"We better get going." Jack rubbed his hands together.

"I'm hurrying." I turned on the light in my closet for better visibility, and felt a heavy tug of desire to back out. If I'd only listened to the voices of reason in the first place. The murderer, my mom, my gut; everything had been telling me to give up and I didn't. My adrenaline had peaked; fear was replacing courage. I tossed my hiking boots out of the closet as I rifled for warm layers of clothing and my green goose-down hooded jacket.

"What does this guy look like, anyway? Is he big?" Jack asked.

"Assuming it's actually Brandon, and not some other guy throwing us for a loop, we don't need to worry. He's not a big guy."

"That's good." Jack picked up my boots and sat on my bed to unlace them. "Hopefully he's only up there with Kaya and not some crew of criminals."

"For sure." I stepped out of the closet, removed my jeans, and began to slip on some wool long johns. "Do you think a thick pair of sweatpants would be warm enough?"

Jack shook his head. "This guy's a moron to think a city girl could make it out there alone in winter."

I turned to grab my sweats. "Unless his goal is to have Mother Nature kill me before he does."

CHAPTER THIRTY

A full hour behind schedule due to road closures, we parked at the base of a dead-end street where the concrete turned to gravel.

"Ready?" My body stiffened, bracing itself for danger.

Stepping outside the SUV, my hiking boots sank into a muddy snow patch. A strike of lightning cut through the darkening sky warning us to turn back. Somewhere in the distance, in a place we couldn't see, the air collapsed in on itself, its invisible gray waves slamming into one another, loud and hard.

I opened the trunk and pulled out my heavy pack. Jack slipped his long arms into the straps of his and clipped the snap on his waist. We were sharing his only set of hiking poles, but anticipating a loss of cell service, he'd printed out the maps, so at least that was to our advantage.

"Go back in the car and wait with the taser." Jack looked at me with pleading eyes.

A fearful inner voice begged me to comply. *Let him take over. You don't have to do this.* Instead, I peered forward. "Not a chance, Jack Miller." I'd caused this problem. There was no way I could let him take the risk on his own.

Ahead, dark shadows cast by fifty-foot cedar trees lurked on the long straight, uphill trail. Menacing silver snow-capped granite cliffs towered in the foreground. A leaden mist began to fall. My stiff boots pounded with each step I took toward the trailhead. "Let's move while we still have some daylight."

"The first three miles are the easiest," he said, matching my stride. "After that, the trail shoots straight up, about 1,300 feet in a single mile."

"Awesome." My voice dripped with sarcasm.

I needed to stop smoking. Five minutes in and my lungs were already exhausted. As if the universe wanted to throw down a greater challenge and remind us it was only going to get harder, the sky closed in completely. Swollen storm clouds unleashed their fury.

Ice cold rain poured in thick sheets, pelting the patchy fallen snow as we ascended the Devils Punchbowl in silence. I hunkered down into my shoulders, pulled on my hood and snapped it below my chin to keep it from blowing off.

The consequences of my decision to come here twisted my future. They affected my family. And they could harm the man who was risking his life to be with me.

Running through the logistics of the plan in my mind, I called out to Jack over the rush of rain, "What time is it?"

"Close to 5 o'clock. We've got another three hours or more to go. If we don't hurry, we won't make it in time."

The path ahead coiled into steep staggering switch-backs. Dense thickets of trees blocked out any remaining moonlight. Jack clicked on his flashlight. Its bright beam cut through the darkness and illuminated shards of silver rain blowing almost horizontal.

He was right, a city girl didn't belong out here, especially in the cold heart of winter. My thighs blazed in agony and my feet were screaming. Blisters were forming. My lungs felt as if they'd been lit on fire.

Thick mud suction-cupped my feet to the ground, coating my boots in layers of slippery sludge. The traction was nearly gone. I jammed my hiking pole deeper into the ground and used it for leverage to push ahead. Even in three layers of clothing, including the snowboarding clothes we'd borrowed from Jack's roommate's girlfriend, it was astonishingly cold.

There was no time to rest, but I was already terribly fatigued. "Go," I ordered myself out loud. "Take another step, Shelby. Charge!"

My heart pounded at the exertion. I paused once, leaning my hands on my knees, allowing my lungs to suck in solid oxygen. Then I stood straight and raced to catch up to Jack, blinded by the beating rain. A river of overflow rushed the path.

"The water is washing away the trail," he called out. "Stick to the sides. It's safer."

The faster I trudged through mud and snow, the thicker the rain fell. Keep going.

The Devils Punchbowl trail managed to grow steeper. A branch ripped at my hair and I let out a tiny shriek, whipping my head back. I could hear brittle limbs snap. Another branch clipped my face. I lost my footing and fought to keep myself upright.

"Are you okay?" Jack shouted over the rainfall.

"I'm fine."

He slowed and I felt his gloved hand reach out for mine. "Let me help you." Our fingers linked as he pulled me forward. "We're getting closer."

Twenty . . . thirty . . . forty minutes later . . . I was freezing despite our vigorous charge uphill. My bones hurt from the chill.

That's when I saw it.

Farther on, to the right of the path, I spotted a dim light illuminating an open meadow. It looked like the kind of clearing where hikers could set up camp. "Jack, look." I stopped and squinted, shading my eyes from the driving rain. "Jack," I reached out, grabbing his shoulder, trying not to yell in the open air.

Near the back of the clearing stood a small shack, a blurry light burned from within. "There." I pointed.

The rain nearly swallowed the tiny wooden structure, as if it would crush it and take it down in the storm. Thunder clapped, and a bolt of lightning lit the night sky, a long, jagged line of white electric fire.

The crunch of snow. The splash of a muddy stream. Jack's hand brushed my heavily padded shoulder. He tugged off his gloves and reached for his gun, racking the slide.

An abrupt click and it chambered a round. "Wait here," he said, "I'll go find the entrance."

CHAPTER THIRTY-ONE

"Jack," I shouted out in a whisper. "I'm the one he wants. Let me go instead." He was stalking the kidnapper alone and I needed to stop him.

Icy raindrops fell softer. They patted my cheeks as I tried to make out Jack's shadow in the darkness. He was either ignoring me or didn't hear my words.

Either way, I listened, fully alert to the sound of his footsteps squishing in the soft mud and forest debris. The edge of his silhouette materialized against the faint light of the cabin as he stepped into the small clearing.

Blood rushed in my ears. Jack crept several more feet ahead. Following behind him, I hid myself in the shadows of the tree line. The killer could be watching. Who else could be responsible for the light shining inside a shack in the middle of the wilderness.

Jack stepped closer into the glow spilling from the shack. I caught the glint of his silver-gray gun, saw him flip off his hood for better peripheral vision.

Holding my breath, I removed my gloves and braced my hands, ready to fight if I needed to. I willed Jack to take cover. This was exactly what he'd told me not to do alone. If the killer was near, Jack was making himself vulnerable to an attack, which meant I would have to be the one to rescue him, and he had the gun.

The rain came to an abrupt stop. A frigid wind picked up in its place and pushed at my hood. Cold air crept down my neck, shoulders and back, making me shiver.

Again, I heard footsteps. But this time they belonged to someone else, someone coming from the cover of the trees. My head whipped left as I homed in on the sound.

Heavy breath riffled the freezing air, the way mine had when I was hiking. My body tensed in terror. I crouched, waiting like a doe in the woods, certain she's being hunted.

I heard a whooshing sound, and spotted something small pierce the dirt beside Jack. As my brain tried to reason why a bird would fall from the night sky, it hit me. It wasn't a bird; it was a dart.

I held in my scream, careful not to draw attention to myself, or worse, distract Jack. The whizzing sound came again, followed by a sharp thwack into a tree trunk. Water droplets pelted the leaves and pattered to the ground below. "No," I whispered, rigid and terrified. My heart was already racing forward before my mind could muster the courage.

Another whoosh. Jack jumped back, gripping his neck and shouting. From the shadows emerged a man's stout figure rushing through the mud in dark clothes. Jack stumbled, trying to gain footing but, by the time the attacker made contact, Jack was out before he could connect with a swift punch to the face.

My heart seized. What if Jack was dead? I pulled out my taser and pointed into the trees, ready to attack.

More rough punching sounds of a heated struggle echoed in the vastness of our solitude. Then silence. Feet dragged out of the tree line and toward the shack's lit window.

I needed to do something. Bolting toward them, I shrugged my heavy pack from my shoulders, the release giving me speed.

"Stop," I called out, several feet away, out of reaching distance and trembling with fear. "Put him down or I'll shoot."

A man dressed in all black stood behind Jack, dragging him through the mud. My insides froze. This attacker was stealthy, and he had the advantage over Jack, just like when he killed Daphne and Melissa in their sleep.

Jack slumped in the dirt, blood covering his face. He coughed and my heart burst open. He was alive. We still had a chance.

"I said *stop*," I repeated, pointing my taser at the man's face. I hoped it looked enough like a gun for him to not notice my bluff. If he'd stepped any closer, I would paralyze him with electricity.

Narrowing my eyes, I homed in to take the shot, making a silent plea. Please let this work. Let this be the end of it all. I'll give up smoking. I'll listen to my mother. I will be kinder to Jack. Just let us get out of here alive.

Aiming for the right side of the man's shadowed face, I pulled the trigger. He dodged. I missed.

"Damn," I hissed, backing up, making sure that my front faced him. I couldn't put my back to him, I couldn't let him get the advantage. I tried to yank the prongs out of the taser to reach the stun-gun underneath.

His gaze ran the length of me. As I fumbled with the

taser he dropped Jack to the ground with a wet thud. Mania pushed into his eyes.

The man's hood fell back when he jerked, confirming what I'd suspected. It was Brandon, Liberty's fiancé. "It's really you," I whispered.

He shook his head and flexed and unflexed his ungloved hands. Pulling his hood over his face again, he covered his skin with his winter coat. I couldn't stun him through a down jacket.

"Why are you doing this? Where is Kaya?" I tried to control my trembling limbs.

"Why am *I* doing this?" he shouted, spreading his legs into a wrestling stance, balancing his weight back and forth like a predator. "You're trying to destroy my life."

My eyes darted to the window and back to Brandon. "Where's Kaya?" I repeated, "You said if I came, you'd release her. Is she tied up in there? Did you hurt her?"

He lunged at me and I jumped back, tripping over a root nestled into the mud. My heavy jacket tightened around my body, dirty water soaking into the fabric. I tried to kick at the ground, but my boots slipped in the slime with each thrust forward.

Before I could make it up, Brandon reached out, hooking my torso. I wrestled, kicking us both forward. His body slipped on top of mine, jostling my healing ribs. I yelped out in pain and he gasped from behind me.

I could smell the alcohol on his breath, feel the shake of his nerves. Breathing heavily, vibrating with adrenaline, I thrashed back and forth, fighting hard to throw him off me as we struggled in the mud. His grip was too strong.

My cheek and then my forehead scraped against the

ground, my nostrils filling with liquid dirt. "Get off of me!" I lifted my face for fresh air and cried out. "Jack!"

"He's out." Brandon panted, his lungs wheezing. "I shot him up with Propofol. I'm not as stupid as you think."

"Then at least let Kaya go. You promised." Tears fell down my face as he held me captive on the ground in a bearhug, tightening his grip while I struggled for release. I should have never suggested Jack and I come out here on our own. We should have done what he wanted and called the police.

Brandon coughed and hocked up phlegm. "Kaya's not here," he breathed hot in my ear. "That day in the park, after the interview. We met with her, Liberty got Kaya's number and set up an interview. She told Kaya she wanted to show her how we'd be honoring Melissa at the wedding."

If what he said was true, Jack and I had come here for nothing else than to get killed. I walked right into his trap and dragged Jack along with me.

Brandon pinned me down. I couldn't budge under his weight. He panted from above me, trying to catch his breath. My energy was fading, I couldn't fight hard.

"So she was safe this whole time?" I snarled, "Is Liberty in on this too or are you the only one who's a total psycho?"

"Liberty doesn't know. Melissa was trying to break us up, Liberty is the only person I have, the only friend, the only girl who ever loved me, I can't lose her. I only went over there to talk to Melissa."

"With a knife? In the middle of the night?" I thrashed to no avail. "So, what, you had no other choice or something?"

"Liberty knows I'm a good man. Melissa and that dumb slut, Daphne, went crazy on me. I had to defend myself." He squeezed me tighter. "You think you're so special? You have to stick your face in everyone else's business. I gave you plenty of chances to leave and you had to keep pushing."

Brandon gasped, pressing a knee into my gut and levying himself up. He grabbed my hands, dragging me to my feet and pulling me toward the shack. "You did this to yourself. You're going to die because you decided you could mess with me."

I went cold at the word *die*.

Kicking and flailing in protest, I still couldn't hold my own. He managed to yank me inside. The shack consisted of one small space, maybe five-hundred square feet. Dozens of mismatched free-standing pillar candles sat arranged in a wide circle, lighting the room. No sink, no lamps, no real furniture.

Neat stacks of circular ads featuring coupons for discounted milk and buy-one get-one-free cartons of eggs lay near a worn green sleeping bag, unzipped and adorned with several pillows. He lugged me toward a tall, sturdy metal and canvas camping chair.

"What is this place?"

Brandon leaned close to me, his stringy hair brushing mine. I yanked my neck back, not wanting to get any closer to the maniac.

"Sit down." He shoved me into the chair. "If you move, I'll shoot you here. Your choice."

He leaned in close, his whiskey breath hot on my lips as he held my hands down. "What'll it be? Are you going to be a good little girl or are you still going to try to play like you're a hero?"

A fresh wave of revulsion boiled in my veins. I was no hero. I was nothing more than a total disappointment. All I ever wanted was to prove that I could take care of myself and help others. Instead I was pinned down in the middle of nowhere, helpless and destroying the lives of everyone I cared about.

The fight with my mom riled my nerves. *Selfish*. She'd always thought I was a spoiled unworthy brat. And she was right.

I'd never done anything exceptional. I'd tried, and failed. I'd cheated on the only man who ever sacrificed for me. And now, thanks to my stupidity, this piece of trash lording over me was going to kill us both.

"Go fuck yourself." I spat in his face.

Staring at me with those wild eyes, Brandon raised his arm and balled his hand into a fist. My head buckled at the force of his hit. Shock dulled the pain. As my vision blurred, and the room seemed to turn itself sideways, I could feel blood dripping from my left temple.

"You're lucky I didn't shoot you in the face," he hissed.

I held myself stiff as Brandon raised his left hand and ripped yellow reflective rope from his jacket pocket. I stayed frozen, keeping a gap of distance between my body and the chair as he looped rope around my arms and torso. Given the chance, it would allow the wiggle room I needed to escape.

"What are you going to do to Jack?" I asked, balling my hands into fists and holding them against my thighs, creating extra space between my forearm and my body.

"You know, I kind of feel bad for him. What's that song? Never fall for a whore? He was trying to do the right thing for the wrong woman. He's a good guy, he doesn't have to suffer when he dies. But you, I want you to be wide awake when I burn you."

My stomach flipped in uncontrollable fear. I swallowed hard, trying not to vomit. For now, struggling would only make things worse.

I took a deep breath and watched the cheap wax candles flicker and wave, leaving a trail of blackened heat in their wake. "Burn me? So I can suffer? You really are sick."

"It'll look enough like an accident once the snow clears in a few months."

Brandon made one final loop around my arms and torso and began to tie several knots. "Big interview, live TV, wouldn't put it past you to decide to celebrate. Maybe Jack left you a little love note with cabin directions, you know, *Devils Punchbowl, tonight at 8*. Maybe you got to this shack and thought you'd spend the night. Maybe you lit candles and fell asleep."

He cut off a fresh line of rope, moving down to tie my legs to the chair. I kicked out at him and smashed into his shoulder. He lost his footing and then found his balance. Back in a kneeling position, he slapped me hard against the cheek, stunning me.

"How's your dad by the way? I see those boxing lessons paid off about as much as the rest of anything else you've had people do for you. Your boyfriend shouldn't have picked a girl just playing games while she waits on her fat inheritance."

I could feel my eyes grow wide in fear. He was zeroing in on my family. What if it didn't stop? What if once he finished off Jack and me, he went after my parents?

"You and your man will both be so badly burned, they'll barely be able to identify you."

"No one will believe I came out here willingly in

December," I said as he returned to tying my legs to the chair.

"No one would believe you'd get a *Good Morning USA* interview either."

Ignoring the increasing ache in my head, I nudged my chin toward the pile of circular ads. "What's up with the coupons?" I needed to keep him talking, to distract him from his task while I figured out a new plan.

"They're accelerant for the fire I'm going to set. Too bad, too. I built this place myself. I'm going to miss it."

"You did a stunning job," I said, mocking him.

"I was an Eagle Scout."

"I bet you dropped out after your third Boy Scout meeting. Your fiancée must think you're a real stud."

He flinched in what I guessed was acknowledgment of the truth, and pulled the rope tighter around my ankles. "She did when I replaced her silver engagement band with your grandmother's wedding ring."

"What?!" I hissed. I hated Brandon more than I'd ever hated anyone. "A real man would save up and *buy* her a gift. All you know how to do is steal."

"I paid plenty. Those guys didn't knock you around and rip the ring off your finger for free. I had to pay extra for them hiding it on the trail so well. It was worth it though. You should've seen Liberty's face when I gave it to her."

"I'm sure she'd really light up if she knew what you do when she's not around. You're nothing but a loser."

"Better than that sad sack laying outside in the mud. What good is he to anyone?"

"Drugging up men with your dart gun is the only way you can get a woman alone. Either that or sneaking into homes in the middle of the night with a butcher's knife to murder anyone who threatens your relationship. How's it feel to be so pathetic?"

"I wouldn't know." He stood up and walked toward the door. "I'm going to grab your boyfriend."

My fear flung into overdrive. "Leave Jack out of this. Please," I begged. "When he wakes up, he won't have any idea who knocked him out. You didn't identify yourself on the phone. Any of the evidence, your cigarette butts at the crime scene, as long as you don't get a DNA test it's all circumstantial. You can leave the country, change your name. He doesn't know you're the killer. Nobody has to know you're the killer."

"Bargaining? Really, Shelby, you're better than that. You still think you're smarter than me. But don't forget, you're the one tied helpless to a chair." As he turned to leave, he scuffed his brown hiking boot to kick over every single candle. One, by one, by one.

Brandon opened the door and a rush of cold air blew in, blowing half the candles out. The remaining flames danced inches above the floor, flickering and swaying in the tiny wooden space.

Keeping watch on the flames as they teased the floorboards with their heat, I pumped my shoulders up and down, and wriggled my torso in desperate violence. Searching for give, I needed to force the ropes down my chest and onto my narrow waist.

I tried to kick my ankles at the chair and rocked back and forth. If I could knock myself over, maybe I could collapse the camp chair's legs and shimmy out an escape.

Jack's backpack and gun flew in through the door and landed with a whack near the center of the cabin. Brandon dragged Jack inside and dropped him before picking up two of the candles and holding them against the sleeping bag until a decent flame started to grow.

Next, he knocked over the stacks of paper ads and left a trail from the sleeping bag to the wall. "You'll be lucky to last ten minutes." Brandon nodded, tipping a chin at me. "From all of us at *NBC 4 News*, Goodnight, Shelby Day," he snarled with his mad-dog expression before strutting outside. The door slammed behind him.

Heat erupted. Fire burned up the sleeping bag and raced across the circular ads. It climbed the far side of the wall in a V-shaped pattern. Flames snapped and spit. A dime-sized ember shot free and landed on my right cheek before burning itself out.

"Jack," I called out. "Jack, wake up."

He lay motionless.

Closing my eyes, I tugged and wriggled my torso and thrust my ankles in quick sharp bursts. I thought of the way Jack looked at me whenever we were together. The deep rumble of his voice. The thick scar that ran from the seam of his bottom lip to the top of his chin, and the gentle way he insisted on spending the night at my apartment to protect me even after I'd told him I'd betrayed him by sleeping with another man.

My senses sharpened. There was only room to focus on survival. At my most vulnerable, the animal instinct to thrash in resistance fully unleashed. I let out a scream so singular and primal, I was certain God himself could hear. I was fighting for my existence. For Jack's existence.

Freedom or death. In a flash of blinding pain, the rope slipped, I felt the release. I wiggled my arms free and leaned over to undo the knot securing my legs to the chair.

Worse than throwing open a burning oven, my skin was already baking in the intense heat. The sharp scent of scorching wreckage assaulted my senses. Jack and I were roasting alive.

The contents of the room; the sleeping bag, pillows, backpack, and circular ads, were fully ignited. Hot air and gasses collected at the ceiling and started banking down. All at once, the ceiling and upper walls exploded into lashing flames. The shack was engulfed in fire.

CHAPTER THIRTY-TWO

Free of bondage, I crawled across the hot floor, coughing in black smoke and reaching for Jack. I stumbled across his gun and tucked the warm metal into the elastic waistband of my pants. Reaching out, I felt Jack's leg.

I grabbed his ankles and struggled with every bit of my might to drag him to the door. The ceiling began to cave. Large chunks of burning wood crashed down above Jack's head. Panting and struggling to stay conscious as the last remaining breaths of oxygen burned, I tugged harder, moved him faster, then turned the handle and flung open the door.

In a blast of fresh air, one last tug, and we were outside. I locked my arms under Jack's armpits and pulled him away to safety.

———

Brandon was out here. I could feel his eyes, watching me.

"Jack." I set him down at the edge of the clearing, a seemingly safe distance from the burning shack. "Jack, are you okay?"

His head flopped to the side. I watched his eyes flutter open and then close. It felt like we'd been out here in this damp lonely wilderness for days, like this nightmare would stretch into forever.

I yanked my mud-caked hood over my neck. Images of Brandon ambushing us from behind or shooting me in the neck with that homemade dart gun flashed through my mind. "Jack," I whispered in his ear, trying to shake him awake. "Jack, please. You need to wake up so we can get out of here." My eyes scanned the tree line, searching for the enemy.

Adrenaline pulsed through every molecule in my body keeping me hyper alert to sights and sound. Brandon was out there, watching. I was sure of it.

Our only advantage was, he didn't know I had grabbed the gun. If I could draw him out, we'd have the element of surprise on our side. Otherwise, Jack and I were easy victims waiting to be snuffed out.

"I know you're there," I called out to Brandon. "Why don't you man up and finish the job? If you let us get away now, you're one-hundred percent cooked."

A branch snapped somewhere close by as the shack's blackened skeletal remains extinguished in the cold winter air. My limbs shook so badly, they hurt. Brandon was approaching.

Kneeling in the mud, I clutched my ribs, pretending to be hurt. I turned the safety off in silence. The bullet was already chambered, I pulled the pin back in my hand.

Fear bubbled in my stomach. The gun weighed down my hand. I had to hold it up. I had to aim straight.

I prayed I could follow all the steps correctly. First time shooters didn't have good aim. I needed to do everything right.

Whoosh. A menacing hiss passed my ears before a dart pierced the ground nearby me. "You missed, moron." I taunted him, hoping to throw off his game.

The sounds of a jacket rustled. Feet hit the soft mud. I spun around and caught Brandon's shadow against the tall trees in the fire's fading glow.

"You can't knock me down." I shouted. "Shoot at me again. I dare you."

Silence. I waited, crouched in front of the fire. Fresh waves of rain unleashed, pouring down my hair, dripping into my clothes, and freezing me to the core. The wind shrieked through the trees, chilling my bones. Brandon held his silence.

A silver glint flashed in the light of the moon exposed by parting clouds. It was a knife. His weapon of choice. Brandon was running at me, charging at full speed. Racing into close range.

He was going to kill me. Right now. And he was going to make it personal.

My nerves burst through my body, terror racing through my veins. I shot up, the revolver clutched within my hands. I lunged my arms into full extension, punching the gun through the night air until it was at eye level. I balanced myself with one knee firmly planted in the mud and the other bent forward. In the heat of panic, I aimed straight for his chest. My hands trembled, the trauma of battle taking its toll.

My finger slowly pressed against the trigger before pulling back in one long smooth motion. My breath slowed. Time stood still. I took aim.

Fire!

Brandon let out a cry and then a whimper as my bullet made contact with flesh. He lurched, gripping his chest, but still storming forward. I shot again.

Another bark of pain. He went down. I'd hit him twice.

The knife dropped to the ground and Brandon followed with it. I waited for him to lie still and then I turned to Jack.

CHAPTER THIRTY-THREE

A wide picture window overlooked the spread of dark-blue waves tumbling toward the shores of the Pacific Ocean. I'd seated myself at a seaside table for two beside a towering Christmas tree in the cozy warmth of San Diego's historic La Valencia Hotel lobby. Taking in the spectacular views behind me while sipping spiked cinnamon eggnog, I waited impatiently for Jack to arrive.

So much had happened since our fateful night only two weeks prior, the night we hiked back from the Devils Punchbowl. When Jack finally came to, aside from a black eye and a throbbing headache, he was fine. We worked together to try and carry Brandon out of the woods.

Two shots. The first one to the chest, the second to the shoulder. He was already in trouble before the second connected. I tried to help him, tried making a tourniquet, but he was bleeding out.

Less than halfway down the trail, Brandon's body went limp and he lost a pulse. We laid him on the path and stormed toward the trailhead for help. By the time paramedics arrived, he was dead.

Next came interviews with the cops, court mandates to return for any further questioning, and my mother flying out to hustle me home. It was such a whirlwind of relief, guilt, confusion, and gratitude, all I could do was text Jack goodbye.

Now it was Christmas Eve in Southern California. Chandeliers adorned with forest-green wreaths glittering in pink, silver, and gold decorations, lit the Spanish-tiled entryway in a soft glow. I kept watch for Jack's handsome face, checking my phone often in case I'd missed a text from him. Nothing.

I'd begged Jack to move back to his hometown, to accept a job as a photographer beside me at the news station where I would begin working next month. It was a two-hour drive from LA, I could visit Dad every weekend. I'd secured the position on Jack's behalf and assured him I was ready for a real relationship. As much as commitment scared me, almost losing Jack had frightened me a whole lot more. He'd agreed and we decided to rent an apartment together and give it a real go.

Checking my cell once again, I shot him a quick text.

Me: Where are you? It's almost 1 o'clock. It's going to get cold out soon.

Jack: Patience.

Me: LOL . . . I'm missing that virtue.

Me: Huuuuuuurry.

It was another one of those moments I cursed my promise to give up cigarettes for good. The rush of nicotine was the only thing besides Jack that calmed the edge. Luckily I didn't have to wait much longer.

I could sense his approach before I saw him. The tumble of the ocean, the clinking of silverware in the hotel lobby, even the hustle of waiters and waitresses, all felt lighter, more at peace.

Jack rounded a corner from inside the lobby. Rocking dark jeans and a worn pair of leather dress boots, Jack's outfit instantly made me feel underdressed in my casual black tank top and blue jeans. But none of that mattered. When we made eye contact, my limbs vibrated with energy. Jack's full lips lifted in a smile like he held a secret.

"Hey, sexy," I smiled back at him. "Look at you all dressed up. What's the occasion?"

"Oh, just some girl I'm supposed to meet up with."

I bit the edge of my bottom lip with nervous anticipation. "I don't think I've ever seen you wear any other shoes besides Vans."

"I wanted to look good for you." He leaned forward for a hug, wrapping me in a welcoming embrace.

My cheek pressed against his black button-up collared shirt. "This is such a cool surprise. You could have waited, though, until I found us an apartment to rent. You didn't have to make the trip out here twice."

He held me at arm's length so he could look me in the face. "Shelbs, it's Christmas Eve. What's the best holiday of the year without my girl?"

I twirled a lock of my hair around my index finger. "Well, I'm excited to finally meet your dad and brother. Tell me again why you wanted to connect here first? Are you stalling out on introducing me to your family?" I asked, looking around the luxurious beachside hotel once again. "Or are they here with you?"

"My dad and brother are at home. They're both eager to meet you."

"Cool." I nodded my head. "I thought maybe we could walk around town and check out the beach. It's so pretty here."

"We will. I need to show you something first."

"What is it?" I asked.

"You have to follow me."

"I love surprises." I bit my lip again, dazed by how extraordinarily nervous I felt. I glanced back at the table. "I was going to order a quick snack to go with my eggnog. I can just leave it though, or do you want to get something to eat first? I'm kind of starving." My head was so buzzed with anticipation, I almost couldn't think straight.

Jack chuckled. "Let's get you food. No one wants to see you hangry."

"No kidding!" I lifted up on my tip toes and gave him a kiss on the cheek. "It's so good to see you, Jack. I'm psyched you're moving here. It's crazy, but I know it's going to be good. These last two weeks away from you have been torture. All I've wanted to do is be near you." I glanced over at my eggnog again. "Maybe we should go check out your surprise. I can order a snack later."

"No way. Eat first." He pulled the low-slung heavy orange leather chair out for me and then waved the waitress over.

As soon as she left with our order, Jack leaned across the table to take my hand.

"Have you heard anything new from Sergeant Dunbar?" I asked. "It's been such a whirlwind since I left, I haven't had a chance to track him down in the past few days."

"They interviewed Liberty."

"And?"

"She didn't know anything. Brandon had her completely under his thumb, she believed anything he told her. Kaya already told the police Liberty had cut her off before work and reminded her about the secret interview they had scheduled to discuss her wedding. Liberty had no idea she was keeping Kaya busy just so we'd believe Brandon had really kidnapped her." Jack nodded a thank-you to the waitress as she set down a small cheese platter along with beer.

"What do you think will happen to her now?" I asked.

"She's got to live her life. Take each day as it goes. The sad thing is, after Dunbar told her that Brandon had claimed he'd gone to 'talk' to Melissa to ask her not to break them up, Liberty claimed to fully believe in Brandon's innocence."

"You think she actually buys that he murdered her best friend by accident? Why would she believe that when she knows he tried to burn us alive? That's total BS."

Jack placed a slice of gouda on a slim cracker and handed it to me. "She's been through a lot. She lost a best friend and now a fiancé, all in a matter of months."

"I guess you can lie to yourself about anything if you really want to believe it."

"Fortunately, the families don't have to sit through a trial and listen to all the awful details."

I wiped my hands on my linen napkin. "Brandon's gone, they'll have DNA evidence back soon to confirm every-thing. Case closed."

"And you helped make it all happen." Jack beamed at me as if I were a superhero.

"I couldn't have done it without you. We make an exceptional team."

"Two is better than one."

I took some cash from my wallet and laid it on top of the bill. "So?"

He gulped down the last of his beer. "You ready to roll?"
"Yes."

Jack pushed out his chair and reached for my hand.
"Let's do it."

My chest expanded in anticipation. Jack and I walked side by side out of the lobby and down a short flight of narrow terracotta-tiled stairs overlooking tiered levels of tropical landscaping. A small, open lawn spread out beside us on the first level, which overlooked a gorgeous pool below, and the Pacific Ocean beyond.

"My brother used to tend bar at this hotel. They have weddings over there." Jack pointed toward the lawn.

"Great location." I squeezed his hand, hoping he wasn't hinting at anything.

"Check out all the cool bougainvillea and palm trees wrapped in holiday lights."

"It's so San Diego. Are you going to miss the Pacific Northwest?" I asked him. "No more wide-open spaces."

We turned right, heading down another narrow pathway until we stopped in front of one of the hotel's private rooms.

"I'd go anywhere to be with you, Shelby, and I'm not just saying that because I'll be back in San Diego. It's going to be awesome." Holding a plastic card to the key sensor, he opened the door. "I rented us a villa for the night, so we could wake up here together on Christmas morning. But don't worry, I can sleep on the couch if you like. No pressure." He grinned at me. "I wouldn't let you do anything you'd regret."

I smiled back at his joke referring to the last time we slept in the same bed together. "Can I trust you?" I giggled.

"No promises." Jack pushed the door further open, encouraging me to go in.

Delicate music, Halsey's *Without Me*, spilled from the sound system. Stepping inside, my mouth opened in surprise. A roaring fireplace warmed the floral-scented living room. Just beyond, in the loft-style bedroom, pink rose petals were carefully arranged in the shape of a heart on top of the king-size bed's fluffy white comforter. Tiny twinkle lights designed like flower blossoms were strung along the headboard and overhead light. It was beyond extraordinary. "Did you do all this yourself?" I asked in near disbelief.

"I wanted our first holiday together to be special."

"I can't believe you thought to do all this, Jack." Tears welled in my eyes. His devotion was real, and true, like nothing I'd ever allowed myself to experience.

I sat on the edge of the bed, laying on my back and spreading my arms like an angel, reveling in the velvety touch of the petals on my bare arms. "Thank you, Jack."

He grinned and walked over to a black overnight duffel bag he'd left on the couch. Jack pulled out a small blue jewelry box and brought it back before me.

"You mean this villa beside the ocean isn't enough?" I asked, a slight sinking feeling filling my tummy. "I don't need anything more." I propped myself on my elbows and looked him straight in the eyes, silently begging him not to ask any me questions I couldn't answer. "Everything is already perfect."

"I know what you're thinking, Shelby, don't worry." He popped open the box and leaned it toward me so I could see what was inside.

"No." My heart fluttered with astonishment and pure joy. Nestled inside the plush jewelry box rested a thin platinum band. It boasted a small blue, oval sapphire encircled in a halo of tiny diamonds. "My grandmother's wedding ring. How did you . . . "

"The police asked Liberty about it, and she turned it in a few days ago. Your mom faxed some paperwork to the Ashland Police Department and had your ring released to me."

"I can't believe you got it back." I held out my right ring finger, and he slipped the band onto its rightful place. I tilted my hand to the left and right, admiring the flash and sparkle. "You even had it cleaned."

"I wanted it to look brand-new for you. It's almost as beautiful as you are, Shelby."

It was hard to resist the urge to pull him in close and kiss him, but there was more I needed to say.

Jack spoke first. "I can't wait to get back in the water and start our new adventure together."

"That'll be great. I'm excited to watch you surf." I took in a deep breath. "Jack, I need to tell you again, how sorry I am for hurting you. I made so many mistakes. So many things I can't take back."

"We almost died, Shelbs. You risked your life for me." He shook his head as if to say I was fully forgiven. "You showed me how much you cared when you dragged me out of a burning cabin, and then again when you got a job for me here so we could be together. Besides that, I came in prepared long before I met you, Shelbs. You're like my first love, the ocean."

"How's that?" I asked.

"Merciless and unpredictable, unforgiving; you can't turn your back on her."

My palms warmed into a light sweat. "That doesn't sound very good."

"But she gives you so much, too." Jack's voice gently rumbled. "She gives you food, she gives you surf. Beauty. She is life."

"After all we've been through." I leaned closer. "Nearly losing you, nearly losing our own lives, I finally understand how much I need you in my life Jack."

"Do you realize you accomplished every single goal you set for yourself in Ashland? You stood on your own two feet, you proved your worth as an investigative reporter, and you helped solve a double homicide. You're kind of the most awesome person I know, Shelby. Not bad for the little rich girl from a big city who nobody believed in."

Blinking back tears, my body flushed with gratitude. "I love you, Jack." This Lost Girl had found herself.

"I love you, Shelby." He placed his hands on my hips and gave me the kiss I'd been waiting for. "I've loved you since the first days I met you. Thank you for bringing me home."

In adult fiction, check out an excerpt from Holly Kammier's International, Best-Selling Novel, KINGSTON COURT:

Natalie: May 22, 2014

I loved the Gaslamp Quarter at night. Here I got to wear heels instead of New Balance, trade my sweats for a little black dress and red lips. The city made me sexy.

It was a tranquil Thursday in late spring and I should have been hanging out with my mommy friends on Kingston Court. Once a week, without fail, we met up in the cul-de-sac with our kiddos in the evening to drink wine and catch up on all the neighborhood gossip. Tonight was special, though. I had a date with my favorite man.

My husband, Mark, shifted the gears of our BMW as I peered up at the passing lights and giant fashion ads painted on the brick walls of San Diego's classic building facades. Victorian-era architecture mixed with modern skyscrapers. The din of traffic and dingy smell of the streets made me forget to worry over ladies' night or our two children at home. At least for this moment, we were young again.

Mark slid a hand against my bare thigh as we slowed at a light. "Wanna ditch dinner and find a dark alley?"

The subtle streaks of his graying hair were hidden in the dimly lit sports sedan, turning him into a darker, more mysterious version of himself. I laughed and leaned toward him, kissing the freckle below his ear. "Tempting. Very tempting. If I wasn't so hungry, I might take you up on that."

I breathed in his citrus scented aftershave, as I wrapped my hand around his bicep. Mark flexed his arm and narrowed his green eyes at me. "You sure?" he teased in a low voice, almost like a growl. "I get all crazy when you dress like that."

"Shoot." My eyebrows sank as I glanced down at my open purse. A small green toothbrush sat on top of my wallet.

"What?"

"I have Ben's toothbrush."

My husband and I looked at each other in resignation.

"Jamie is watching him. Maybe it'll be fine," I said, though we both knew it wouldn't.

Our five-year-old son could be difficult. His most recent obsession was brushing his teeth after every meal. I could think of worse things for him to be insistent upon, but going to bed without his toothbrush of choice wasn't an option. It was only a matter of time before my best friend would call, telling us to come home.

Mark's tired face turned stoic without the charm of his smile. He pulled into the next U-turn lane to head back for the freeway.

"Are you mad?" I asked, reaching for his knee.

"Eh, we'll just drop it off and swing by that Thai place you like." He shrugged and took my hand, reverting back to the role of comforting husband.

I scrunched up my nose and removed the barrette holding back my shoulder-length brown hair. We were celebrating my thirty-eighth birthday and there was nothing romantic about the Taste of Thai at our neighborhood strip mall.

The light in front of us turned green, and I brushed my hand against the back of his neck, hoping to be absolved of my guilt. "Maybe we can still—"

He turned to look at me. His eyes, focused only on mine, carried none of the fear I suddenly felt wash over me. In that single moment life froze. I needed to speak, to take the wheel, something. Instead, I watched the set of headlights outside Mark's window get closer.

An intake of breath. A downpour of shattered glass. The sound of my scream as if it belonged to someone else.

The car lifted then, tumbled. A dizzy Ferris wheel of lights . . .

ACKNOWLEDGMENTS

Thanks to Shelly Stinchcomb, Jessica Therrien, and Christa Yelich-Koth for all of your time and encouragement while content-editing my manuscript. Thanks to Laura Taylor and Debra Cranfield Kennedy as well.

Thanks to Lacey Impellizeri, for combing through every single page of *Lost Girl* to ensure each of my millennial characters is authentically twenty-something. Shane Bishop, the national producer for my favorite primetime crime show, for giving me valuable insight into investigative reporting. KOBI Channel 5's owner, Patricia Smullin, and General Manager, Bob Wise, for welcoming me back to my old stomping ground and allowing me to shadow the station's news team. Nikki Torres for giving me an insider's view of how up-and-coming reporters work in the field these days. And to my awesome step-brother, Micah McAllaster, a firefighter engineer and SWAT paramedic, for teaching me a little fire science and about treating injuries.

Thanks to my extraordinary beta readers for all your feedback—Leslie Abecilla, Ken Impellizeri, Daphne Katz, Jessica Ross, Mary Jane Therrien, and Mandy Urena.

I'd also like to thank La Valencia Hotel for hosting my family over Valentine's Day in order to research one of our favorite San Diego establishments.

Thanks especially to my boys for sacrificing your mom's attention and allowing me time to write. You are my greatest pride and joy. And to Julian, thank you for giving me my love story.

WWW.HKAMMIER.COM
WWW.ACORNPUBLISHINGLLC.COM

If you liked this book, please leave an online review and tell your friends. Word of mouth is an author's lifeblood. *Thank you so much for reading!*

CPSIA information can be obtained
at www.ICGtesting.com
Printed in the USA
FSHW020635250719
60370FS